Look Sharpe!

The Valkyrie Series
Caribbean Pirate Adventure

I0530687

by

Karen Perkins

LionheART Publishing House

Published in Great Britain by LionheART Publishing House

Copyright © Karen Perkins 2016
ISBN: 978-1-910115-70-1
2nd Edition

LionheART Publishing House
Harrogate
UK

www.lionheartgalleries.co.uk
www.facebook.com/lionheartpublishing
publishing@lionheartgalleries.co.uk

Caribbean, 17th Century, United States, Pirates, Sea Stories,
Women Pirates, Adventure, Historical fiction, Colonial history,
Caribbean history, African American history, Sailing

Cover Design by Cecelia Morgan

Dedication

For the Louises: wonderful people, great friends

Author's Note

Throughout the Valkyrie Series, I have used the historical and phonetic spellings of place names, and where possible taken these from Edmund Halley's map of 1699.

The Caribbees

Hispaniola

Puerto Rico

Sankt Thomas Island

Sankt Jan Island

St Croix

Sayba

Sint Eustatius

St Christopher

Gadalupe

La Isla Magdalena

Dominico

Martinico

Barbados

Grenadines

Grenado

Look Sharpe!

PART ONE

1678

Chapter 1

I stared at the coffin, the only one not shrouded in dust and cobwebs. *So that's it—I'm alone. Well, apart from Uncle Richard.* I fingered the letter in my pocket; but he was an ocean away, on the same continent as Elizabeth and our child. She had never returned; I didn't even know if she'd had a girl or boy. Hellfire, for all I knew she'd perished on the passage out.

"I heard from Uncle Richard today, Father," I said to the coffin and drew out the letter. "He sends his greetings from Jamaica, although as always he is a little late." I managed a half smile at the weak joke. It was one of Father's frustrations that both my mother and her brother were perpetually tardy, but it was a joke of affection. My mother was ever late now, of course, having passed in childbirth twenty years before. Father had missed her terribly. I still did.

I pulled the candle closer and held the letter to the meagre light.

My Dear Nephew Henry,

It bereaves me to hear of your father's illness, Charlotte thought so highly of him, as I do myself. I beg of you to be good enough to pass on my regards and prayers for swift progress in his recovery.

Life in the Indies suits me well, as I am sure it would yourself should you ever desire to escape England's green shores. Jamaica is a lively island, filled with diverse characters, although regrettably there is a vast shortage of ladies. Some of the four-legged and marine life are just as diverse as the fellows, simply amazing to behold. The color and noise of the place is too wondrous to describe and my door is always open to you, my boy.

Windhaven is successful beyond my most desirous dreams. My sugar cane stretches for leagues in every direction and needs a small army to tend it. The Great House is magnificent, even in comparison to Rowleston Hall, and I am certain you would soon feel at home here.

The only disadvantages are the malodorous airs and the greed of the merchants. They charge abominable rates to ship my sugar, rum and molasses. The situation is so dire, I am considering a venture into shipping myself. Surely funding my own vessel will save me quite a pretty penny.

I must now take my leave, a ship is departing for England's bonny coast within the hour and I must hurry to press this missive into the captain's hand.

Your Loving Uncle —

Richard Tarpington

"I'm going to go, Father," I said, relieved to tell him of my decision, even though he could no longer hear or advise me. "The death duties, added to the other debts, have crippled the estate. I've had to sell off fifty acres to pay everything. Barker can manage the rents and tenancies, keep everything ticking over until I come back. Three years, that's all, Father. Long enough to make my fortune in sugar. White gold they call it. I'll come home in time, buy the land back, and restore Rowleston Hall to its former glory, you see if I don't. Anyway." I pulled myself together, realizing I was asking for approval from a coffin. "I'll make you proud, Father," I added into the silence.

I blew out the candle, then walked toward the square of light and out into fresh air. I pushed the door of the mausoleum closed, locked it, then took out my hip flask and drank a deep draught of brandy.

Unhitching my horse, Maximillian, I swung up onto his back and turned his head away from Rowleston Hall. I turned in the saddle to take one last look at the only home I'd ever known, then pointed Max's nose toward Bristol, the docks, and the New World.

Chapter 2

I sat down at the table and raised my tankard in greeting to the three men I was joining.

I'd been in Bristol a fortnight; my ship, *Pride of the Orient*, was more than a week overdue and nobody had any news of her. I could well be waiting on a ship that rested on the sea bottom, but I had nothing better to do but stay and hope.

I threw the dice. Three. I groaned. I'd lost most of my money. I had nothing left with which to buy my own stake in sugar, and was a little short for my passage out. I had to win tonight. I could ill afford any more aces and deuces.

Like father, like son, I thought. Neither of us could ever resist the dice, cards or anything that resembled competition; or drew bets for that matter. My father's losing streak had killed him. Mine was about to kill my dreams. I threw again. Four. I kept my face impassive. I had to turn this around. I had to.

I raised my tankard again as another man sat down to the dice, threw and nicked.

I'd had enough and stood to leave. The latest addition to the table joined me outside.

"Jonesy." The man stuck his hand out as he introduced himself. I shook.

"Lord Henry Rowleston."

"Ah, that explains it."

"Explains what?" I withdrew my hand, not liking his comment.

"Why they were fleecing you in there."

"Fleecing me?"

"Aye, did you not realize them dice were weighted? You had no chance. You don't go into a tavern like that one with your fancy clothes and wig, calling yourself Lord Summat Or Other, not if you want to keep your coin and that fine cloth on your back."

"What do you mean?"

"I mean, this is sailortown, mate. The people here live tough lives. They're worked like dogs and paid little, they see a gentleman like yourself in their lair, they're gonna take whatever advantage is in their power."

"They were *cheating*?"

"Blimey, that's took you long enough, you're not exactly sharp are you? Aye, 'course they were bleedin' cheating— this ain't one of your poncey gentlemen's clubs here you know."

I stopped walking. "Why are you telling me this? You took a fair bit of my coin yourself tonight if I remember rightly."

"Aye, well. You needed a lesson. I were once a little like you and I'd have ended up in t' gutter with the rats if some kind soul hadn't taken me to one side and explained the way o' things. I'm just passing the good deed on."

"Well, I'm grateful to you, Jonesy. Although passing it on a bit earlier would have been more helpful."

"Aye, well. Men don't like to be told, not when they have a purse full of coin and a plan to win more."

I shrugged, but realized he was right. Dressed in dirty

breeches and shirt, grime under every fingernail, I wouldn't have given him the time of day a week ago.

"Come on, let's have an ale, you look like you could do with a bit of fortification."

Chapter 3

"No. No, no, no, no, no," Jonesy said when I opened the door of my boarding house to him the next evening.

"What's amiss? You said to dress in breeches and shirt."

"Old breeches and shirt."

"These are old."

"Not old enough. Not tatty enough. Not dirty enough. Where's yer room?"

Silently, I led the way.

"Right, breeches first."

I looked at him in confusion.

"Breeches. Off."

"What?" I stared at him. Was he really trying to help me, or was my humiliation at the dice not enough, was he trying to compound it?

He sighed. "What do you see when you look at me?"

I shrugged, embarrassed.

"No, tell me what you see, I won't be offended."

"All right. I see a ruffian, a scoundrel, a scallywag."

He drew himself up to his full height, plucked my wig from its stand and put it on his head, then spoke with a very different accent. "So you would be surprised to know my real name is Fotheringay, and I'm as much lord as you are?"

I gaped at him.

"Hard times, Rowleston, hard times. My family lost everything to bloody Cromwell in the wars. I've had to turn my hand to many a distasteful task since and have learned how to prevent myself from becoming prey. You remind me of myself a few years ago." He removed the wig. I couldn't move for shock. "Now get them bleedin' breeches off," he added in his low-born accent. I hurried to obey.

After we had stomped the muck of the floor and our boots into my clothes and rubbed ash into my hair, Jonesy appraised me once more.

"Aye, that's better, but you can't go round introducing yourself as Henry Rowleston, with or without the Lord." He stood, his hand raised to his chin in thought.

"Sharpe," I said, thinking back to a comment he'd made the night before. "Henry Sharpe."

He laughed and clapped me on the shoulder.

"Aye, Sharpe's the name all right. Let's hope it'll soon be thy nature too."

"Different tavern, different luck," Jonesy said as we entered. I paused and surveyed the room, but nobody had stopped what they were doing to look in the normal manner occasioned by my entrance into one of these places.

"Seems like it," I said, nonplussed at my new anonymity, although I did draw a glance or two as I strode to the bar.

"Sharpe," Jonesy said with a warning look, and I hunched my shoulders a little, kept my voice low when I asked for ale, and dropped a few aitches. Jonesy nodded his approval and we dragged our feet over to one of the noisier tables where the dice were rolling.

*

Three hours later, pockets full, we stepped back outside and congratulated each other.

"The game's a bit different when all's fair and square," said Jonesy.

"Ain't that the truth!" I clapped him on the back. "I owe you, Jonesy, I can't thank you enough."

"I told you, passing the kindness on. I've done nothing for you that wasn't once done for me."

"Still." I held out my hand and he shook it. "I won't forget."

He nodded, then his eyes widened. I spun on my heel and drew my knife. One of the men we'd rolled with stopped in his tracks.

"What can we do for you, sir?" I was Lord Rowleston, Earl of Shirehampton again, just for a moment.

He started in surprise at my accent, glanced at my blade, shook his head and melted back into the shadows.

"Aye, you're a sharp one all right," Jonesy said. I laughed and we staggered back to the boarding house.

Chapter 4

As had become my habit, my first duty after breaking my fast was to take a stroll to the docks and inquire after *Pride of the Orient.*

The wharves had been built where the River Avon met the Frome and, looking out over the water, all I could see were hulls and spars. I stared for a moment, as I always did, marveling at the skill involved in bringing these ships to rest amongst so many without wrecking.

"Watch it!"

I stumbled backwards as a runaway cask careered toward my legs, just managing to avoid it.

"Begging your pardon, watch out!" a young boy cried as he chased it down on its path to the next unsuspecting pedestrian.

I shook my head at the chaos and continued my trek to the coffee house to meet with the Merchant Venturers.

"Lord Rowleston."

I turned at the shout and greeted my accoster. "Jonesy, good morning to you." We shook hands. "What are you doing here?"

"Ah, just watching the shipping and dreaming of faraway lands." He gave an embarrassed laugh, then continued, "No Henry Sharpe today?"

I grinned. "No. Some things, at least, are better done as an earl." I indicated the harbor with a jerk of my head. "My ship has come in, I'm on my way to the Venturer's Rest to speak to the owner, pay my passage, and claim the best berth for the voyage."

Jonesy nodded, but said nothing. I realized I would miss the man; he had been a good friend to me in the short time we had known each other. "Why don't you join me?"

He shrugged. "Got nothing better to do today, I suppose."

We wended our way past stacks of casks waiting to be loaded; crowds of people, also waiting to be loaded I presumed; and tangles of hemp and canvas.

"I'll wait out here," Jonesy said when we reached the coffee house. "I'm not dressed proper for this type of company."

I hesitated, then nodded. "I won't be long."

Business transacted, I blinked as I stepped outside. The sky was overcast, but still seemed hellishly bright after the gloom of the interior of the coffee house.

"All done?"

I nodded at Jonesy. "It will take them five days to unload. Then they'll swab it out, erect the cabins and load supplies. We leave on Wednesday next."

"A little over a week." He looked despondent, then confused and the corners of my lips tugged upwards. "Hang on. We?"

Now my lips stretched wide. "Yes, we, you're coming with me."

"What? But . . ."

"Those faraway lands you were dreaming of? We'll be standing on their shores in about seven weeks from now."

11

"But . . ."

I raised my eyebrows in question. "But what? What's keeping you here? You're alone, earning a living at the dice table. There's a whole new world out there, let's see what it will give us."

I could see him getting ready to "but" me again, then his brow smoothed, his eyes sparkled, and his shoulders straightened.

"Aye," he said. "All right, mate, you've a deal. But I'll pay you back the cost of the passage."

"No you won't, yer daft bugger," I said, slipping into Sharpe's vernacular. "If you 'adn't taken me under your wing when you did, I'd be penniless now. I only 'ave the money for the passage 'cause of your intervention. I still don't 'ave enough to buy into my uncle's sugar plantation, but no matter, our fortunes 'ave changed, we'll manage it somehow."

Jonesy laughed. "The New World. The Caribbees, here we come!" He grabbed me in a bear hug and spun me round, both of us giggling like girls now. People gave us a wide berth and strange looks as they passed us: the gentleman and the ruffian. I didn't care. I'd be traveling after all and in the company of a friend.

Chapter 5

I shrugged off my frockcoat and stared around in horror at the tiny gloomy space I would have to call home for the coming six weeks. I hung my coat on a nail then stretched out both arms. My fingertips brushed each "wall"—in reality a flimsy partition of wood—as I swayed with the floor.

"Jonesy?"

"Aye?" The answer floated, clearly audible from next door, over the six-inch gap at the top of the wall.

"What in hellfire is that canvas thing?"

"Judging by the lack of a cot, I can only assume it's a bed, Sharpe."

"A bed? But how the hell do you stay in it? How the hell do you get in it in the first place?"

"Hmm."

There was a pause and I tugged at the loop of cloth suspended from the deckhead. A grunt and a crash made me jump.

"Not like that!" Jonesy laughed.

Alarmed, I rushed next door. "Are you well?"

"A little bruised, but well enough." Jonesy extended his hand. I took it and pulled him off the deck. He stood before the bed, hands on hips, then said, "Maybe if I roll?"

He clambered in sideways, rolling over as he did so. "Got it!"

Laughter escaped my throat despite my despair at our sleeping arrangements. "How will you sleep like that?"

"I'll have you know it's very comfortable," he said, voice muffled.

"Can you turn over?"

"I'm not sure I want to risk it."

I laughed again. "A crown says you'll tumble."

"A crown you say?" He lifted his head and arms and wriggled. At least no longer face down, he still looked extremely uncomfortable twisted on his side.

"All the way if you want the crown."

He grumbled, but resumed wriggling.

"Aha," he exclaimed, then, "No!" as the material swayed and tipped him to the deck.

I held my hand out to him again, this time with palm open to claim my winnings, then spun round at a loud guffaw at my back.

"Out of the way, gentlemen, I'll show you how it's done," said the man, one of the crew by the look of his weathered face and muscled arms, still laughing at Jonesy's antics.

I raised my eyebrows at him and he stopped laughing.

"Tom Little," he introduced himself.

"How d'you do, Little?" Jonesy called from the floor and I helped him up. "I'm Jonesy, and this here's my good friend, Lord Rowleston, Sharpe to his friends." I nodded at the sailor. "By all means, show us how to get in these infernal things," he continued.

I stepped aside and Little squeezed into the tiny space.

He reached up and found a handhold in the beams above, then jumped up, swung himself across, lay back in the hammock, and sighed in satisfaction. "Nothin' to it, sirs."

"See, Jonesy? Easy!" I mocked as Little jumped back down. "My thanks, Little, you've saved our bruises and further embarrassment."

"Any time, sirs."

Jonesy held out his hand and something shiny passed between them.

"That better not have been my crown, Jonesy."

"For no bruises and embarrassment? 'Tis cheap at the price."

"That was my winnings!"

"Winnings you say?" Little butted in. "Do you gentlemen enjoy the roll of the dice, by chance?"

Jonesy and I glanced at each other.

"We have been known to occupy ourselves with the dice on occasion," I said, hesitant, or at least hoping to appear that way.

"Well, if either of you are at a loose end during the passage, there's usually a game to be found on the lower deck, near the bow. Tell 'em Little sent ya."

"Our thanks, Little," Jonesy said and shook his hand. I smiled and nodded at him, but spotted a smirk as he turned to leave. I watched him head to another "cabin" that had just emitted a loud thump and a curse, then turned back to Jonesy who was rubbing his hands in glee.

"We need to take care," I said, and told him about the expression I'd seen on Little's face. "They'll try to fleece us."

"O'course they will. We're traveling in style, they think we're rich and simple just like that night we met."

I frowned.

"But we know their game, we'll suck 'em in, take their money and spit 'em out again!"

"Care, Jonesy. There's nowhere to go and very few places

to hide. Don't forget we're aboard a ship, their ship. Play them too hard and we could end up overboard."

He slapped me on the back. "Ah, Sharpe, ever the cautious one. Let go, live a little, take a few risks."

"What the hell do you call this?" I waved my arms to indicate the ship. "This is the biggest gamble of my life! I'm leaving behind everything I know, with no idea as to what's ahead, and you call me cautious?"

"Aye, you've a point there. Come on, let's go up on deck, get a last glimpse of Bristol."

I nodded, then stumbled as the ship jolted beneath my feet.

"Don't fret, it's the anchor coming free of the bottom," Little called out from somewhere to our right.

"Come on, Sharpe, hurry," Jonesy said, leading the way back up to daylight.

Chapter 6

I breathed deeply, and wondered just how foul the air would get in our sleeping quarters.

"Come on, Sharpe, mate, out of the way."

I moved from the hatch to give Jonesy some room and apologized. A team of sailors worked at the bow pushing a capstan round to haul the anchor aboard, and I glanced up in unease at the still-furled sails.

I turned to look at Bristol; the wharf a heaving mass of people, warehouses, and traveling and boarding houses crammed in higgledy-piggledy behind it. The River Avon was full of ships in various stages of preparation: being unloaded, loaded and made ready for sail; the water itself full of all manner of flotsam and jetsam. I wrinkled my nose in disgust at the smell and sight of sewage floating past.

The sailors at the bow cheered as the anchor broke free of the water and the ship moved sideways, the bow slowly swinging round.

"Helm to windward."

"Stand by to fend off."

"Why aren't the sails being used?" I grabbed Little's arm in panic as he passed.

He laughed, enjoying my fear. "Wind ain't steady, it

swirls around like a doxy's skirts here. Even worse in t' gorge. Tide's stronger and will take us out."

"But, but, how can the captain steer without the sails?"

"Can't, not by much." He grinned, then took pity on me.

"Then why doesn't he have a boat out to guide us through?"

"Don't fear, sir, we've a pilot aboard, he does this every tide, and it's a strong tide, too fast for the boats. Sails are next to useless till we hit the Severn."

He pulled away from my grasp as I winced at his use of the word hit.

After a few more shouted commands and a number of jarring bumps against other ships, we were in the main channel and racing seaward.

"Ladies and gentlemen," the captain (at least I presumed he was captain) called, and I wondered if he ever spoke in a normal tone of voice.

"Welcome aboard *Pride of the Orient*. I hope you find her comfortable." There were a few mutterings at this. "I realize the accommodations are not what you are used to, but they are the finest any oceangoing vessel out of Bristol can boast."

"'Tis a feeble boast, man, my slaves can tell of better!"

I craned my neck, as did Jonesy and everyone else to see who had spoken, but he perchance regretted his comment and fell silent.

The captain frowned and did not respond to the insult.

"The passage will take a little under six weeks given fair winds, please feel free to walk the decks but mind my crew. Your lives are in their hands for the coming voyage and I advise you keep that in mind in your dealings with them."

A few more mutterings. My heart sank; this was not

shaping up to be a pleasant voyage, I had already taken a dislike to a number of the dozen gentleman and even one or two of the ladies who stood complaining on the deck.

"We'll be out of the shelter of the gorge soon, and when the wind picks up it'll be coming from larboard." He pointed to his left. "If you feel ill, I recommend the starboard rail." He pointed to his right, then turned his back on his passengers to confer with one of the sailors.

"Not much of a welcome aboard, was it?" Jonesy remarked to the man standing next to us.

"Hmpf," he grunted and turned away.

Jonesy shrugged his shoulders. "Friendly ship," he said, and I laughed.

"Hopefully people will be a bit friendlier once they're settled in and have got over their nerves."

"Nerves? What do they have to be nervous about? It's a fine ship with, you heard the captain: 'accommodation of the highest standard'."

"Are you serious? Crossing an ocean to a new land in a ship this size and no one to help us if we find trouble? Hellfire, I'm not bloody nervous, I'm downright scared and so should you be." I stopped when I realized Jonesy was laughing at me.

"Just playing with you, Sharpe, trying to ease the tension."

I frowned and pressed my lips together. My belly was fluttering with fear at what may lie ahead; both at sea and after our arrival at Jamaica, assuming we made it. I was not in the mood for jokes and as I gazed at the lulling waves my mind drifted back in time. *Heavens, it must be ten years since, and yet seems like yesterday—a part of me I'll never forget and will always regret.*

19

"Henry."

I turned at the shout, searching the crowd for her. A pale arm waved above the sea of hats and bonnets. Elizabeth. I pushed through the throng. I'd found her.

She stepped into my arms and I held her close, aware of the faint swell of her belly against mine, then buried my face into her mass of curls. I'd been distraught when she had disappeared and had interrogated the other maids and servants to finally find the truth. My father, the Earl of Shirehampton, on discovering our affair and Elizabeth's condition, had arranged passage to the New World. He would not countenance the thought of the next Lord Rowleston being the father of a kitchen maid's bastard at seventeen years of age.

"I thought I'd never see you again."

"I couldn't let you go without saying farewell."

She pulled away from me, a look of horror and despair marring her delicate features. "Farewell? You're . . . you're not coming with me?"

I took hold of her hands." I can't, you know that. My father, the estate . . ."

She pulled her hands away. "What about me? What about our child? You told me you loved me, that you'd never forsake me."

I hung my head in shame. "I do love you, Elizabeth, I do. But I have a duty to my father and family name. When he's gone, then I'll be free. I'll come and find you. Keep our child safe and I'll find you."

She stared at me, her large beautiful eyes full of pain. She did not believe me.

I fished in my pocket and pulled out a necklace. A large amethyst teardrop hung from a fine chain. I opened the clasp and held it up to her. She did not move. I fastened it around her neck. She did not take her eyes from mine.

"It was my mother's." My fingers brushed the stone now resting on her chest. "The love we share is impossible, but that does not mean it is not true. I love you, Elizabeth, but I have to let you go."

Still she did not speak.

"You're embarking on a new life, in a new land. You can be anybody you want to be there, in America."

A tear fell and caressed her cheek." I want to be with you. I want to be your wife."

"You know that can't happen. Not here. An earl—even a courtesy earl—and a maid cannot marry in England and have any kind of meaningful life. We would be ridiculed and shunned, our child would have no prospects."

Elizabeth hung her head, tears dripping freely now. I pressed a fold of banknotes into her hand, then gripped her shoulders, and planted a kiss on her crown.

"I'll never forget you, Elizabeth. Never."

She nodded, picked up her valise, turned and was soon lost to me.

My senses were overcome by the hustle and bustle of the docks, but I stayed where I stood, my feet rooted to the dirty cobbles.

The mob of humanity thinned as the pilgrims and émigrés boarded the great ship anchored in the River Avon, and which would take them a world away.

"Standby at the braces."

I jumped at the captain's shout and wondered what was happening. Crew men ran to positions by the tangle of rope that stretched from mast to hull and I glanced ahead with trepidation. The high cliffs sheltering the river were diminishing to nothing and the water was a wholly different color only a cable's length ahead.

As sails unfurled, another shout rang out. "*Haul to leeward.*"

Sailors released some ropes and hauled on others as the wind hit. *Pride of the Orient* lurched over a couple of waves, then settled into a new rhythm.

I joined the rush to the starboard rail, the churning in my belly suddenly too violent to ignore. I swallowed a couple of times, but knew what was coming and emptied the contents of my stomach into the Severn. My wig was whipped off my head and I grabbed for it, knocking Jonesy's arm. He released his hold and I watched my hair drift alongside for a moment, then it was in our wake and gone. I punched Jonesy's upper arm in frustration.

"What the hell, Sharpe?"

"What do you mean? I thought the wind had taken it, not you, what were you doing?"

"Trying to save the cleanliness of your curls, mate."

"Nice job," I replied through gritted teeth, "they're well and truly washed now."

"Aye, well, I guess that's it for Lord Rowleston, ain't it, Sharpe?"

I didn't answer, but hung my head over the side again. I'd worry about the wig later.

Chapter 7

Three days later, I lay in my hammock and wondered if I should try to exit it. With Little's guidance I had managed to get in, but had not yet attempted the reverse procedure.

I sniffed and groaned. The stench down here was unbelievable; the buckets that served as pisspot, shittenpot and of course vomitpot were nearly full. Jonesy had reckoned, on one of his brief visits, that near a score of my fellow passengers were similarly affected.

I grabbed the side of the hammock and shifted my weight. I reached the deck a little earlier and harder than I had intended, but I had made it without upsetting the bucket. Good enough; I'd have plenty of time to practice my technique.

I clambered to my feet and staggered, regained my balance, then fell against the walls. A little foul-smelling liquid slopped out of the bucket and I realized that had been happening for some time.

I picked the bucket up by its rope handle and held it away from my body as I made my unsteady way to the steep stairs and quickly worked out that balance was easiest to attain with feet planted wide apart with each step.

A rather awkward, one-handed climb—complete with a little more spillage—later and I was in fresh air. I lifted my face to the breeze and breathed deeply. Heaven. A slight, fresh aroma of salt tingled my nose and taste buds.

"*Sharpe.*"

I turned at Jonesy's shout and headed toward him. "No! Other rail," he called and pointed to the other side of the ship.

"Some daft bugger emptied his bucket to windward," he said when he joined me. "Emptied t' bucket into the wind and covered his face and chest, and those of his wife, with the contents!" He laughed, but I grimaced. They would have little chance of being clean again until we made land. Water was a precious commodity aboard ship and there had already been numerous arguments about the amount rationed to drink, even by those who had been suffering from seasickness. There would be no water for washing until the next rainstorm.

"Good to see you on your feet again, mate." Jonesy slapped me on the back.

I groaned. "Have a care, Jonesy, everything's still a little . . . unsettled."

"Oh, sorry." He stepped back a pace and I grinned.

"Maybe you need something to take your mind off your belly?" Jonesy added. "That Little and his mates play a mean game of dice."

"Maybe later. For now I need fresh air, water and something solid to put in my belly."

"Oh, aye, o'course. Sorry, mate, things 'ave been a bit quiet with you laid up."

I nodded. "Where's the kitchen?"

"Galley, mate, galley. We're at sea now."

I stared around me in surprise. I had been so

preoccupied with my stomach I had taken no notice of my surroundings. I turned in a slow circle, amazed.

"There's, there's nothing there," I told Jonesy.

"Nope, just sea and sky," Jonesy replied, indicating the horizon. "Just sea and sky to look at for six weeks."

I smiled. I quite liked the sound of that.

Karen Perkins

Chapter 8

"That's not our dice!"

"It damn well is," Jonesy shouted back.

"*No*," Abbots insisted. "Look, it's bigger than the other."

"Are you calling me a blackguard?" Jonesy jumped to his feet as he shouted, and cracked his skull against the deckhead.

I drew my knife and stabbed it into the wooden barrel top between Little's fingers.

"Make one more move toward his or my own coin and you'll lose a finger," I warned.

Little withdrew his hand and Jonesy sat down.

"You were trying to steal from me?"

Little shrugged. "You've cleared me out, we'll be sighting Jamaica soon. I've a woman there who likes silver."

The group of men huddled around the barrel burst into guffaws. I stared at them, then glanced at Jonesy. This hadn't been one man spotting an opportunity to help himself, but two: Abbots had caused the distraction. I wouldn't have been surprised if all of them had been in on it. We gathered our coin.

"Well, I'd like to say it's been a pleasure, gentlemen, but this game is turning a little sour. It's time for us to go up on deck for a little . . . fresh air." Jonesy said, and we stood, stooping to avoid the wood above our heads. We had spent most of the past six weeks down in this dank hole; sweating and stinking, huddled around a barrel doubling as gaming table. Things had been genial up to now; I guessed we were nearing the end of our voyage and the crew wanted back the coin we had won from them as well as that we had carried aboard.

"Not so fast," said Whitey, the largest and burliest man of the group. "Little here has made his apologies."

I cocked an eyebrow at this.

"I heard no apology," I said, "only excuses."

"Well, that's as may be," Whitey continued, "but apologetic he be, ain't that right, Little?"

Little nodded a vigorous assent.

"We've all been mates for the past month or so, there's no reason to fall out now."

"No reason?" Jonesy asked, incredulous. "No reason? We've given you ample opportunity to win our coin, you lack the skills to do so and attempted to steal it from us instead!"

"Law of the sea, mate," Little muttered, and the rest of the sailors laughed.

"Aye, on a pirate ship, perhaps," I said, wincing at the "aye"; a month and a half in the company of Jonesy and the sailors had proved decidedly unhealthy for my linguistic capability.

The sailors laughed, the tension broken.

"Land oh. All hands on deck."

The shout carried down through the decks to our ears and the men stood, shoveled what coin they had left into their pockets and, with a sarcastic tug of the forelock by Little and a wink from Abbots, they rushed topside.

I looked at Jonesy, more than a little bewildered. I had been prepared for a fight and suddenly had no adversaries.

Jonesy shrugged. "We're here," he said. "Let's go have a gander."

Chapter 9

I wiped my face and blinked more sweat from my eyes, then waved my hand to disperse the cloud of flies for a moment. The sun was fierce and far hotter than anything I'd experienced before.

I shielded my eyes with the flat of my hand and peered at Port Royal, Jamaica.

It was Bristol in the making. Huge warehouses, filled with God only knew what treasures; brick-built mansions, three or four, some *five* stories high above the sand; and I even spotted the spire of what could only be a cathedral rising above it all. The wharf was piled high with goods: huge casks, filled with sugar I presumed; piles of animal skins tied with twine and stinking in the sun, even at this distance; enormous tree trunks which I guessed was the logwood that provided the deep red, purplish color so enamored by the ladies of England. And everywhere was hustle and bustle. Small boats filled so high with goods that their gunwales only barely cleared the water were being rowed out to the ships. Empty versions of the same proved the profitability of their trade. So this was "the richest and wickedest city in the world".

Over to the left, a large, empty space was filled with

lengths of rope and I realized the Jamaicans had established their own ropewalk. Huge wheels spun and twisted the tremendous lines of hemp, and I was amazed that so much had been achieved and established in little more than twenty years.

Our trunks were lowered into one of the small rowing boats and I glanced at Jonesy. "Are you coming, mate?" I asked with a concerned smile. He stood stock still, staring at the town built on white sand and turquoise water. He looked terrified; a state of being I had not witnessed in him before.

"What's wrong?"

He shook himself out of his reverie and turned to me. "It's just so . . . different."

I laughed. "What did you expect? This is the New World, I hope to God it's different to the old one!"

Jonesy managed a smile. "I know, I just didn't expect it to be *this* different." He swatted a hand at the reformed swarm of flies hovering about our heads and hitched his shirt away from his skin. I grimaced and did the same with mine. There had been no opportunity to wash our clothing in fresh water for almost a month and everything was stiff with salt. It was bad enough when first donning a seawater-washed shirt, but half an hour in the oven of the holds playing dice and it was sodden, itchy and extremely uncomfortable. Ten minutes in the baking heat above deck was enough to sweat, dry and sweat it through again; our attire was hardly recognizable as sartorial.

"Come on, stop worrying. This may be Jamaica, but it's still English, man, they're waiting for us in the boat."

Little, on his best behavior when, as now, he was in view of his captain and first mate, tugged his forelock after casting our little boat off from the mothership, and I gave him a friendly wave that in actuality was the complete opposite.

I didn't personally know the sailors at the oars, and relaxed as we moved away from *Pride of the Orient*, Little and his shifty mates.

I clambered up onto the wharf, closely followed by Jonesy, and looked about me.

"There." I pointed to an inn with a depiction of horses displayed on its frontage. "We need to hire horses and get directions to Windhaven."

Jonesy nodded and we dragged our trunks to the waiting establishment. After a couple of very welcome jugs of ale in the relatively cool interior, and with my pockets considerably lightened, a cart containing our trunks stood at the ready with the ostler's young son at the reins. Two horses, saddled and bridled, shifted their hooves behind it. We crossed to them, unhitched them and mounted.

"Lead the way, lad," I called, and our little caravan moved off into the island's interior and the unknown.

I prayed for a friendly welcome; it had been many years since I'd set eyes on my mother's brother. I'd been a child when he'd last made one of his rare visits home. I'd been fascinated by his stories; he had been part of Cromwell's expedition, the first official sailing to the New World, and Mother had often warned Uncle Richard as his tales of cannibals, boucaniers and fierce savages grew too lurid for my young ears.

Admittedly, deep down I was grateful to her. I remember I had always suffered nightmares after a day spent in the company of my uncle, but had always hankered after this faraway place of which he had been so enamored.

I glanced into the lush green forest on either side of the

track. Strange noises emanated all around, and I jumped at a particularly loud cawing and a flash of bright color, then sighed in relief; not a savage, but a tropical bird.

I caught Jonesy's eye and he chuckled. I frowned. *How has he recovered his equanimity so quickly? Our surrounds are now far stranger than at the docks.*

"Windhaven," our guide called and guided the cart between two great stone pillars. I glanced at the name etched onto the stone and felt a shiver of excitement; how often I'd dreamed of this moment.

I looked ahead, eager for a glance at the house, but could see naught but tall plants swaying in the gentle breeze: sugarcane. I itched to stop and taste some, but, with a glare at the cart pulling ahead, I decided to wait.

"You there! Out of my way. Goddamn you!"

Startled, I broke into a trot to catch up to the cart and was shocked to see the young lad still berating men on the track; men who were many years his senior.

"What's the problem?" I asked.

"Nothin' to fret about, sir," the young lad replied. "Just a bunch of lazy negras in the road."

"Since when do you speak to or about your elders with such disrespect?" I demanded, and the boy jumped in surprise.

"Elders? They're slaves. Animals. Don't waste your respect on them, they're nothing."

I stared at him, then turned in my saddle to look back at the men we had now passed.

Thin and wiry, with skin glistening in the sunlight, the man in front met my eyes and I shuddered at the dull despair I saw there.

"Welcome to the New World," Jonesy muttered beside

me, and I glanced at him, my excitement at finally reaching Windhaven having dissipated.

We passed through a bend in the track and at last I had my first glimpse of the house. I was disappointed; I had expected something grander. Uncle Richard had boasted it was fit to rival Rowleston Hall. *He must have had a different property in mind*, I mused, staring at the squat, single-story wooden building. It had an air of neglect about it: greenery growing wild, paint peeling, even a shutter hanging off at a window.

A man came out of the front door and stood on the veranda, hands on hips, watching us approach.

"Richard Tarpington," I called. "Where is he?"

"Who's asking?"

"Lord Henry Rowleston-Sharpe," I said, combining my two personas. "His nephew." I was annoyed, *Does no one on this island possess any manners?*

The man visibly started, then approached, his frown smoothing out into a welcome smile.

"Harry Stanton," he said, "at your service, My Lord. I'm afraid you've had a wasted journey. Mr. Tarpington is not here and isn't expected for some time."

"Why? Where is he?"

"Wherever the wind has blown him." I frowned at the man and he added, "Aboard the *Edelweiss*. He puts into Port Royal regularly. If the ship's there he'll be somewhere about."

Chapter 10

"You knew, didn't you? You and your father."

The boy shrugged. "Not for us to say."

"You didn't want to talk yourself out of the hire, more like," Jonesy added.

"We just hire the horses to them that asks, and drive the carts to where we's told."

"Leave it, Jonesy," I interrupted. "I would still have come out here to see for myself."

He glowered at me and I shrugged. I couldn't see the point of getting irate over something that couldn't be changed.

Jonesy huffed and said not another word until we were back with the ostler, who raised an eyebrow yet failed to look surprised.

I glanced at Jonesy to stay his grumbling, and dismounted.

"No luck, I'm afraid. Do you know if Richard Tarpington's ship, the *Edelweiss*, is here?"

"The *Edelweiss*, is it?" The man perked up and glanced at his son, then jerked his head seaward. "Aye, she's the one at anchor over yonder, that one off to the left with the three masts."

Jonesy humpfed and the man glanced at him warily.

"For all I knew, your man was at Windhaven. His ship's in, isn't it?"

"Of course, don't mind my friend here. Can you kindly direct us to the best boarding house on the seafront?"

"That would be Mrs. Sue's, hundred yards down that way."

"Where you goin', boy?" Jonesy demanded. "Them trunks won't take themselves."

The ostler glanced at Jonesy, then myself, and nodded at his son, who sat himself back down with a grimace of protest.

"My thanks." I shook his hand, remounted my horse and followed the boy to Mrs. Sue's.

"Tarpington? Never heard of him," Mrs. Sue responded when I inquired of my uncle. I nodded and looked around the room Jonesy and I had taken. Two cots, a washstand, and our trunks took up most of the space. Basic to say the least, although it felt like luxury after six weeks on *Pride of the Orient,* even though it was as hot as an oven. I threw the window wide and drew in a lungful of fresh air; if dockside air could ever be called fresh.

"You'd best take care with the window, especially at night," Mrs. Sue remarked. I turned an inquiring eyebrow to her. "Flies," she said. "Little fighting ones—makes sleeping a bugger. You'll be right when you've got used to the heat. Anyway, I'll leave you to it, got bread in t' oven."

She bustled out of the room and Jonesy and I looked at each other.

"You know the best thing for this heat?"

"Ale," I replied, and we laughed.

"Shall we inspect the local taverns?"

"Aye, let's do that."

We chuckled again, I shut the window and we made our way outside.

"Sharpe. Jonesy."

I peered through the clouds of tobacco smoke from myriad clay pipes to see who had called our names.

"Little," Jonesy said. "Why's he being so friendly?"

"Let's find out," I replied, and led the way through the crowd of carousing sailors. Even a man like Little could pass for a friend in a room full of strangers.

He stood in a crowd watching half a dozen men at the dice "table"—another upturned barrel. Everyone held their breath as the next man rolled, then roared their approval at the double six and his shout of, *"Nick."*

"Fancy joining them, Sharpe?" Little asked.

"Not if you or your mates are in any way involved," I retorted.

The men around me, including Little, laughed, and a few amused glances were sent my way from the men seated at the game.

"Well, you've some sense in your head, at least, boy," said the older man, his voice sounding as grizzled as his face looked. He threw, and the audience groaned.

Little shrugged. "'Twasn't me who done the cheating."

I'd had enough. I was not going to let my name be maligned any further.

I pulled my dagger and held the tip to his throat. Silence fell on the men and game around us, and people backed away to give us space.

"Lord Rowleston-Sharpe," I said slowly, dragging my name out for effect, "does not cheat. Nor do his friends. I thank you to keep that in mind and would be grateful if you would educate your mouth to that effect. You have maligned my own character as well as that of my friend. You tried to steal from us. One further misplaced step and my blade will not stop at your throat. Do you understand me?"

He started to nod, thought better of it, and said, "Aye. Beg your pardon, Lord Rowleston."

I grunted acceptance of his apology and withdrew my knife. Little backed away, and the game restarted.

"Lord Rowleston-Sharpe?" the grizzled player asked.

"Yes," I said warily. No one could know the name, not an amalgamation of my true moniker and my pseudonym.

"Henry?"

Comprehension dawned. "Uncle Richard?"

"Well I never. Look at you all grown up. Landlord, more ale, make it your best and keep it coming! My prodigal nephew has arrived!"

The crowd cheered, whether for us or the ale I wasn't sure.

"Less of the Uncle Richard, boy. Tarr or Captain is the only way I want these men to think of me, understand?" he instructed quietly under the noise.

I nodded dumbly, shocked by the menace in his voice as he whispered this aside. I glanced up at him and, although the eyes were a color and shape I remembered from boyhood, their expression was cold and hard, and could not have been more different from my childhood recollections. What had happened to Uncle Richard to turn him into Captain Tarr?

Chapter 11

I blinked my eyes open with a groan, then a yell as I swayed violently on my attempt to sit up. The Brazilian bed, or hammock as the sailors aboard *Pride of the Orient* had called it, tipped me unceremoniously on the floor; no, *deck*, I realized.

"*Hellfire and damnation.*"

"Good morning to you, Henry."

"Wha—?"

"Welcome aboard the *Edelweiss*."

"The what?" Images from the night before flickered through my mind. "Uncle Richard?"

Richard Tarpington strode into view. Face weatherworn from years under the tropical sun, untidy whiskers, brown eyes the color of good, fertile English soil and the same brown of my mother's eyes, the only thing I remembered of her. His dress was tatty: breeches, shirt and hat. He was barefoot.

Jonesy would be impressed, I thought, then said aloud, "My mate, Jonesy, where is he?"

A sound akin to the grunt of a hungry pig sounded behind me. I turned in time to see a hand flopping back into another Brazilian bed.

I realized I was still sprawled in a heap on the floor—deck—and made to get up, only to bang my head on the wood, which had lurched beneath me. At least, I think it had lurched; or was I still addled?

Uncle Richard laughed and offered me a hand. "It's a bit choppy today, but you'll soon get your sea legs."

Sea legs? Choppy? Understanding dawned. "Are we sailing?"

My uncle guffawed so loudly, Jonesy's head popped up out of the folds of canvas to see what was going on.

"Do you not remember putting out to sea, lad?"

I shook my head, then quickly stopped the movement and put a hand to my pounding temple. "No," I said, as substitute for the gesture.

My uncle laughed again.

"Do you by chance have water, Uncle Richard?"

"Aye, and plenty of it." He passed me a beaker and I drank greedily, immediately feeling slightly better. "So, Lord Henry Rowleston-Sharpe. That's quite a mouthful."

I made as if to nod, remembered my affliction in time and spoke instead. "Aye." I winced, I was really going to have to take more care over my speech or I'd end up talking like Jonesy and the sailors.

"I take it from the 'Lord' that your father has passed?"

"Yes, three months ago now. I did write . . ."

Uncle Richard shook his head. "Never reached me. It's a bit difficult to collect letters when at sea most of the time. My commiserations to you, lad, he was a good man." This time I did nod; blast the pain in my skull. "So, where did the Sharpe come from?"

I told him the story about Jonesy and the games of dice in Bristol.

He nodded and remarked, "Sounds like you've got a

good mate there, one with an intelligent head on his shoulders." Another porcine grunt emitted from the occupied Brazilian bed.

"Where are we headed, Uncle Richard?" The repercussions of the fact we were sailing had just hit me.

"Wherever the wind takes us, lad." He laughed at the horrified expression I'd been unable to keep from my face. "Sayba, lad, the island of Sayba, with the blessing of a wind fair and fresh. And I told you last night, boy, I want none of that Uncle Richard malarkey. It'll win you no favors with the crew to keep reminding them you're family. You'll call me Tarr or Captain when aboard the *Edelweiss.*"

"Why Tarr?"

"Tarpington's a bit of a mouthful, like Rowleston. And it reminds the crew I'm a cut above them. Tarr makes me one of the men, they have more respect for me as Tarr than Tarpington." He chuckled at my amazement. "The majority may be Englishmen, but this ain't England, lad, her fine and fertile lands are far away. In the Caribbees it's every man for himself. It's deeds that earn respect out here, not names. I'd advise you to drop the Rowleston, too, stick to Sharpe, Henry."

"Aye," Jonesy grunted from his canvas pit.

The implication of this struck me. "So we're staying aboard, then?"

Uncle Richard—Tarr—chuckled again and shook his head. "You've no head for rum have you, lad? You and your mate there," he nodded toward Jonesy, "signed me articles last night. Both of ye's part of a privateer crew now. Mrs. Sue were none too happy though, to lose her lodgers so soon."

"Privateer? Mrs. Sue?"

"Aye." He pointed to the side of the room; no, cabin. I kept forgetting we were at sea and the rolling of the floor—deck—was real and not down to my addled state. I squinted and made out the shape of our trunks. I crossed to the only unoccupied chair in the cabin and sat down, my mind a blank, unable to process the events of the morning so far.

"What's a privateer?" I asked eventually. "Is that like a pirate?"

"No, it blasted well isn't!" Tarr roared. "Pirates are scum of the seas, robbing and killing with no impunity. Privateers are licensed and perform a vital service to our merry monarch, King Charles."

Jonesy mumbled something and Tarr narrowed his eyes. Thank the Lord he hadn't heard what was mumbled: By robbing and killing *with* impunity.

"*Edelweiss* is commissioned by Henry Morgan himself, the acting governor of Jamaica, and the best privateer Jamaica has ever seen. England may be at peace with the Netherlands, France and Spain, but that won't always be the case. Morgan's put us in league with a couple of Dutchman in Sayba, but France and Spain's ships are fair game, as long as we either sink or commandeer the ships and leave no survivors to give account."

"Dead men tell no tales," I said dully, having heard the phrase in a Bristol tavern.

"Aye, that's it, no bugger can tell a tale from under the sea, can they, lad? The plunder's shared out between the crew and any seaworthy ships taken to Sayba."

"What happens to them there?"

"Refitted, crewed and sailed to Africa. We need strong, healthy men to harvest the sugar."

I thought back to my brief visit to Windhaven and the

man the ostler's boy had insulted in such an offhand manner.

"Slaves? You trade in slaves?"

"Not us, boy, we trade in ships. It's not for us to say how they're used. Those Dutchmen are nasty characters, though. Jan, the elder, is bad enough, but watch out for his son, lad. There's something not right about Eric van Ecken. I've never seen the eyes of a living man look so dead."

A crash made me jump, and Tarr spun round—Jonesy had fallen out of his bed.

"Get him sorted, lad, then I'll reintroduce you to the crew. And no more 'Uncle Richard', understand?"

I nodded and got up to see to Jonesy. *What the hell had we gotten ourselves into?*

Chapter 12

"*Cheval. Here.*"

One of the men dropped the line he was coiling and scampered over to Uncle Richard—I still found it difficult to think of him as Captain Tarr—giving me and Jonesy the once-over; one of the most calculating looks I'd ever seen.

I glanced over at Jonesy, who raised an eyebrow in reply. I didn't like where this was headed.

"Cheval, I have a couple of new deckhands for you to train up. Meet my nephew, Henry Sharpe, and his good mate, Jonesy."

Cheval smiled at us, but I spotted a fleeting glimpse of something else in his eyes before his mouth stretched. *Wariness? Distrust?*

"Welcome aboard," he said, his voice accented with France.

"Cheval will show you the ropes, you'll master the deck before you head into the tops or onto the quarterdeck."

The Frenchman visibly recoiled at the mention of the quarterdeck but I ignored him and smiled at my uncle.

"Don't let me down, boys. It's serious work, Cheval here will show you how to stay safe." He paused, clearly waiting for Cheval's affirmation—which did not come. "Won't you, Cheval?"

"Oui, Capitaine."

"Sharpe here is precious to me." He grasped my shoulder. "If anything happens to him, it'll be your neck I string up."

I glanced between the two men, realizing the first impression Jonesy and I had formed of the Frenchman was shared by my uncle. I narrowed my eyes in confusion. *Why would he put us under the care of a man he does not trust? Is this a test? And if so, whom is he testing, Cheval—or me?*

"You'll need to shed those coats and boots—footing's bad enough in bare feet, never mind leather. Gather by the foremast in two minutes, then I'll show you 'ow to swab the decks." Cheval grinned, turned his back, and sauntered forward.

I raised my eyebrows in question at my uncle. I was a lord for Christ's sake! This Frenchman was having me do the work of a scullery maid!

Uncle Richard shrugged. "No rank aboard ship, lad, unless captain. Everyone starts at the bottom—you'll find your places naturally. I wouldn't keep Cheval waiting, he has a cruel streak."

Jonesy pulled my arm and I let him lead me to the hatch to stow our outer clothing. I glanced back once at Uncle— no. *Captain* Tarr. It was already easier to think that way.

Jonesy nudged me. "Listen," he whispered and glanced toward a gaggle of men at the rail. I stopped pushing the bible-sized block of sandstone over the deck and sat back on my heels, my back popping as I stretched.

I looked over and realized Cheval was holding court over half a dozen men. Even had I been unable to understand French, it would have been clear by the amused smirks and frequent glances thrown our way that Jonesy and I were the subject of their amused conversation.

I caught the odd word as the Frenchman's voice rose. Babysitting, neveu—nephew, inutile—useless.

I made to stand and Jonesy grabbed my arm and shook his head. "Your uncle has done us a service by introducing you as Henry Sharpe rather than Lord Rowleston. We have a card up our sleeve, no sense in telling him we speak French—knowledge gleaned may come in useful later."

I nodded, my teeth gritted, and bent back to my task while keeping both ears primed.

"*Sail oh.*"

I jumped at the shout from overhead.

"Where away?" came Tarr's answering bellow.

"A league off to starboard."

I watched my uncle jump into the ladder of rope leading up the mast—the ratlins—glass to his eye. After a moment he leaped back down, shouting.

"*All hands, clear the decks. Prize to leeward.*"

"You 'eard 'im, clear that away and get yourselves some weapons."

I gaped at Cheval, who laughed. "Welcome to battle. Don't worry, the first one's the worst—assuming you survive it!"

Jonesy took hold of my arm once again and we looked at each other. Neither of us had any words.

"*Go.* Dump that water overboard and put the bibles away. Arms and blades are being brought up. Step to or you'll be left with the duds."

He walked away, still cackling, and Jonesy and I swung into action. Whatever happened now would depend on the gods—and my uncle.

Chapter 13

Standing at the starboard rail, the ship was clear to see. Two masts and a hull low in the water.

"A nice bonus there, lads."

"Little!" I greeted him in surprise. "What are you doing here?"

He shrugged. "Dunno. Seemed a good idea last night when I signed the articles." He looked off to the other ship. "Not so sure now, though."

Neither I nor Jonesy had a reply and we watched the ship draw closer in silence.

"Follow my lead, boy, I'll see you right."

I started at my uncle's hand on my shoulder and could barely hear his words over the cacophony of the crew shouting, *"Kill! Death! Blood!"* in accompaniment to a percussion of weapons striking the rail.

I nodded, my mouth dry.

"Don't mind this," he indicated the bloodlust around us, "it's theatre. If *you're* feeling awed, imagine what that crew are feeling, seeing us bear down on them like this, knowing there's no escape."

"No escape?" Jonesy asked.

"None." Tarr indicated the flag now flying at the top of the mainmast. "Blood red. It tells everyone at sea there'll be no quarter given if they resist.

"And do they? Resist?"

"Not for long, boy. Look at those men—they have cannon aboard. They aren't firing. Just as well, she'd make a good prize to accompany us to Sayba, and she's no good to us underwater. But we board as if they'll fight to the death." Tarr grinned and I recoiled at this caricature of the uncle I'd known and admired as a boy. "Here." He passed us both a long, wide silk ribbon. "Tie each end to a pistol and drape it round your neck. It's easy to bring your guns to bear and your ball won't fall out, even if it's not properly wadded. Probably." He stooped to pick up something else. "You'll need one of these, too." He handed me a grappling hook knotted onto a line. "Throw hard and throw high. Get that secure in their rigging, then swing—just like when you were a boy, eh Henry?"

Still unable to speak in my fear, I could only take the small iron boat anchor and rope. The rope swing I'd used as a boy had been about merriment. This was about battle. Death. Nothing like my boyhood games.

Tarr—I was thinking of him that way most of the time now—clapped me on the shoulder, almost hard enough to threaten an undignified tumble over the rail as our bow cannon exploded with a warning shot. Only Jonesy's steadying hand saved me.

"Keep your wits about you, boy." He raised his voice to include Jonesy and Little. "Your eyes peeled, your weapons handy and your fear in check. You're privateers now, lads—buccaneers. The seas are rich for a man brave enough to help himself."

I nodded, my mouth still arid and lacking coherent speech.

"Steady, men, on my mark.

"Tops—covering fire if you please."

I jumped as muskets fired above, then again as Tarr roared. "*Go*. Throw them high, throw them sweet, we'll be rich men come dusk!"

Screams caterwauled in accompaniment to a multitude of three-pronged iron spikes clanging against each other, then spars.

I'd thrown my own with the others, barely realizing it, and joined my new crewmates in jumping and swinging. I wondered if their screams were for effect or contained as much terror as mine did.

I pulled my blade as soon as I landed, despite falling to my knees, and just managed to parry a blade swinging for my neck. I headbutted the man in the groin, then scrambled to my feet, glancing around to see if anyone had witnessed my ungentlemanly conduct. Cheval grinned at me. *Why did it have to be him?*

My heart jumped when I spotted a man with his eye on Tarr and bringing his pistol to bear.

"*Capitaine*." Cheval shouted the warning and we both took aim—Cheval belatedly due to his call. My ball felled the man before Cheval even got his shot off.

He swung round and stared at me in amazement. "That was a hard shot! But I'd have got 'im myself, you know."

I smiled at his attempt to negate his praise, and looked around for another target. There were none. The crew were overwhelmed and under-armed. We had the ship.

"My thanks, Henry." My uncle shook my hand. "I didn't realize you're such a crack shot, you'll be in the rigging next time with a barrel full of muskets."

" 'Twas an easier shot than it looked, Un— Captain," I hastily corrected myself. I glanced over at Cheval, who had flushed bright red in rage. I smiled at him, amused that he hated the thought of another earning praise from his captain. I flicked my eyes lower, to his hand which still held his gun, now pointed at me.

"Do you intend to use that?"

"*Cheval*," Tarr reprimanded.

The Frenchman's jaw worked furiously—he looked like he was chewing the words he did not quite dare utter. Then he lowered the gun. I laughed as the ball fell from it, unable to help myself in the relief of the fight being over. My mirth proved infectious as the men nearby realized what had happened and joined in. I could almost see Cheval's fury turn to hate and my laughter died in my throat. I had made an enemy this day, and something told me he was not a man to let go of a grudge lightly.

"*Sharpe.*"

I turned at Jonesy's shout, then burst into laughter once more.

"To replace the one you lost overboard at Bristol," he said as he presented me with a perfectly curled periwig.

PART TWO

June 1683

Chapter 14

"Captain?" Blake, Tarr's quartermaster and second in command, prompted, and Tarr tore his eyes away from his intense inspection of one of the ships in Eckerstad's harbor.

"*Down helm. Let go anchor,*" he boomed. A man at the bow struck a pin and three and a half tuns of iron smacked the surface then plunged to the depths.

"*Main topsail aback.*

"*Loose all sail.*"

Amidst the frantic activity of the crew stowing sail and line, Tarr beckoned both myself and Blake to come closer.

"That twinmaster," Tarr almost whispered to Blake. "Isn't she the one we took two months ago off Saint Lucia?"

Blake gave the vessel a close examination of his own. "Aye, Captain, you're right, she is, but she don't look to have been refitted as a slaver."

"No, she's been fitted for speed, look at the rake of those masts."

Blake nodded. They were leaning back at an angle rather than standing straight upright like the other vessels in the harbor, making the ship faster, but harder to work.

"There's not many sacrifice ease for speed," Tarr added. "Them that do are usually privateers, pirates or men-of-war."

"So which is that one then?" I asked.

"Good question. I'm guessing we'll find out soon enough. Keep your eyes and ears peeled today, lad. I don't like the look of this at all."

Tarr, Blake and I dismounted in front of the most ostentatious buildings I had seen since my arrival in the West Indies. It was huge. Built of brick—*where do they get that out here?* I wondered—it had two stories and towers topped with Dutch whatnots at either end of the house. I had thought Rowleston Hall impressive, but this was arrogance beyond belief.

"*Henry.*"

My uncle's voice knocked me out of my reverie and I blinked at him.

"Give Wilbert the horse."

I realized an African man dressed in indigo and gold livery was standing by me, patiently waiting for me to put the reins in his outstretched hand.

"My apologies," I said, and smiled as I passed my horse over to him. He didn't look up, but kept his eyes turned down then led the three horses away, all without saying a word.

"Come on, lads, time to enter the lions' den. Keep your eyes open and your mouths shut. The elder van Ecken is sound enough, but his son scares the bejesus out of me."

I looked at him in surprise, then at Blake, who nodded silently. I faced the house again, nervous now about meeting the Dutchmen.

The door opened and another African man stepped aside

to allow us entry. My eyes widened at the opulence of the entrance hall. Open to the roof—*all that space, wasted*—a staircase fit for any of King Charles's palaces rose before us, then widened to serve both corridors of the upper floor.

"You're expected in the drawing room," the liveried man said.

"Right you are, Hendrik, or is it Hans? I can never tell you two apart. Open the door then!"

The man didn't react, but took our frockcoats and opened one of the two doors leading off the entrance hall.

I flicked a smile at him as I passed, but again, no reaction. *The rules of etiquette are different in the New World*, I mused, remembering the ostler's boy on my arrival. *I don't like it, good manners cost nothing.*

Inside, four men sat on sofas, glasses already nearly empty.

"About time, Tarr," a middle-aged, rather rotund man remarked, and all four stood.

"Sir Henry. This is a surprise," Tarr exclaimed.

"Aye, well, I've been too long in England and neglected my business interests. Who's this?" He flicked his cane in my direction.

"My apologies. May I present my nephew, Lord Rowleston the Earl of Shirehampton, Sir Henry Sharpe. Henry, this is the revered Sir Henry Morgan, Deputy Governor of Jamaica."

Even I'd heard of Henry Morgan: Admiral, Buccaneer, Scourge of the Spanish. He'd been sent to England in disgrace after his attack on Panama; only to be feted by all of London society and King Charles himself, knighted and made deputy governor of Jamaica. He had then turned against his fellow buccaneers, and was responsible for the hanging of scores of former colleagues. A ruthless bastard, currently engaged in a bitter war with the new governor, Thomas Lynch, Morgan was not a man on whom to turn your back.

I bowed. "I'm very pleased to meet you, Sir Henry. Your reputation precedes you, this is truly an honor."

"Hmm. Another Sir Henry, hey? Can the Caribbees bear two of us, do you think?" He turned to include all the men in the room in the joke, then faced me again. "You have a big name to live up to, boy, let's hope you prove yourself. Blake." He nodded a greeting to Tarr's quartermaster, preventing me from making any reply.

"Sharpe," Tarr said, careful not to use my Christian name again in front of Morgan. "May I present Mijnheer Jan van Ecken and his son, Erik."

"Pleased to meet you." I shook their hands. With no title, they did not merit a bow and I was slightly flustered that neither offered one to me.

"And this, if I'm not very much mistaken, is Edward Hornigold."

I nodded a greeting to the man who stood behind Morgan, and he narrowed his eyes at me.

"Aye, the two of ye sailed together, did ye not?" Morgan asked. "All three of ye were with me at Panama. Ah, those were the days." He knocked the rest of his drink back; rum by the color of it. "Right, enough chitchat. Now that you're finally here, let's eat."

He led the way through another door and I noticed the set jaws of both van Eckens. They had barely uttered a word, and clearly did not enjoy being treated as guests— and lesser guests at that—in their own home.

Chapter 15

I was surprised to see Henry Morgan take the seat at the head of the table and Ecken Senior seemed resigned to the foot, but his son Erik looked, to my eye, to be amused at this usurping of his father's position at his own dining table.

I took my seat between my uncle and Blake.

"What's he doing here?" Blake whispered across me to Tarr.

"Hornigold? Nothing good, that's for sure," he replied. And to me he added, "We sailed with him at Panama in '71. It was a nightmare: a jungle road to Hell that Morgan led us down. Hundreds of men died by starvation and Spanish lead, and the rest of us only survived by eating the leather of our belts and boots. And then there were barely any spoils to be had."

I gaped at him as he shuddered; the story he had told in his letters had included no mention that he'd partaken in the destruction of that city.

"Aye, lad, it weren't pretty," Tarr continued in a murmur. "When we finally reached Panama City, them that still lived, anyroad . . ." He paused. "I'm ashamed to say we were all gripped by a murderous madness. Too many people died too many torturous deaths. Aye, some of them at my own hands," he added in response to my unspoken question.

I looked down at the table, unable to meet my uncle's eyes. I didn't know how to react; he wasn't the man I'd always thought him to be. *Had* all *his letters been lies?*

"Me and Blakey here, regret the things we did that day even if they were Spaniards, and it were mainly for nothing. We found no gold to speak of. But Hornigold? Hornigold's an evil bastard. He enjoyed the slaughter, danced in the blood of them townsfolk, and worse. I got him off my crew, first opportunity that presented itself. But Morgan's always had a soft spot for him."

"Aye, that's right, Tarr, and you'd do best to remember it."

All three of us—Tarr, Blake and myself—looked up, startled, into the grinning face of Ed Hornigold. He'd heard every word. He raised his glass in a toast, and I shook my head at the folly of using such a delicate vessel to drink from.

"To Sir Henry Morgan, Admiral of the Fleet, Deputy Governor of Jamaica, and Knight of the Realm!"

"Henry Morgan," the rest of us muttered and drank. I noticed the van Eckens staring at Hornigold in open dislike. I don't think he even realized he had insulted the Dutchmen by proposing the first toast. Or maybe he just didn't care.

The serving girl flinched at Morgan's pat on her behind as she took his plate, then grimaced at whatever Hornigold did to her backside. She moved to the younger van Ecken, Erik, who put a protective arm around the girl's hips and glared at his two guests.

"Gentlemen, shall we to the drawing room retire?" Jan van Ecken stood and asked. It was the first thing he'd said apart from dinner table chitchat, and I began to realize just how much tension there was in this room. Not only between Tarr, Blake and Hornigold, but between the van Eckens and Morgan as well. They did not enjoy having any one of us at their table.

"Aye, well meant, if not well said, van Ecken." Morgan lumbered to his feet and van Ecken flushed at the criticism of his English. "It's time we got down to business." He led the way out of the dining room, and I watched the van Eckens' reactions: tight smiles and gritted teeth. I glanced at Tarr and he nodded as we got up and followed them from the room.

Settled in comfortable seats, delicate glasses of rum in hand, we waited whilst Morgan guffawed something at the girl, his head again out of sight behind her. Jan van Ecken gripped his son's arm so tightly that Erik shook him off.

"Klara, put the jug on the table and leave us. We can help ourselves."

She bobbed a little curtsy and did not bother to hide the relief in her eyes. She almost ran in her escape from the room.

"Sir Henry, maybe you could us enlighten to your plans?" Jan suggested, his speech heavily accented and forestalling any further comment from Erik. "Why is Captain Hornigold here?"

Morgan glared at him; clearly he liked to do things his own way and at his own pace. I felt a sneaking admiration for the Dutchman—the only one who had dared question the legendary buccaneer.

"Hmpf, well," Morgan began. "As I gather ye've not yet heard, that obdurate bugger, Lynch, has finally got his

wish and succeeded in removing me from the Assembly."
Shocked silence fell on the room. *Is he no longer deputy
governor then?* No one dared ask for clarification. "I have
more time on my hands and I've decided to expand our
little . . . venture. Oh, you're doing well enough, Tarr." He
held up his hands to forestall my uncle's protest. "But you
know well enough two ships working in consort have more
success than two ships working alone."

"I take it Captain Hornigold here has the command of
that twinmaster?"

"Aye, the *Freyja*," Hornigold said. "A little beauty she is
too —"

"I know her well, Ed," Tarr butted in. "I was the one who
took her in the first place."

Hornigold said nothing.

"If ye've quite finished," Morgan said, his voice booming.
"The pair o' ye will sail together, Tarr in command."

Tarr didn't react, and Hornigold looked sullen. Morgan
took a long draught of rum and belched.

"The bloody Spaniards have it too easy these days. I
want their ships. I want them running scared of the waters
around Jamaica, if not the entire Caribbees. The West
Indies are English, not bloody Spanish, and the sooner the
stubborn buggers realize it, the better."

I'd heard rumors of Morgan's hatred for Spain, but had
thought them exaggerated. Now I was not so sure.
Apparently the Spaniards thought him some kind of devil,
as they had Sir Francis Drake a century before.

"Surely England's not at war with Spain again," Erik
exclaimed. Morgan turned on him, his face red.

"England may not be, but I bloody well am! And always
will be as long as I've wind in my sails. Do you
understand?"

Erik stared at him, jaw clenched, and said nothing.

"Bring the vessels to Sayba, those large enough for slavers, anyroad. The others can go to the bottom. We only need a small number of men to work a slaver; take volunteers, the rest can sail their ships to the seabed. There must be no survivors to tell tales, understand?"

"Aye." Tarr, Blake and Hornigold nodded. I didn't move, I couldn't believe the callousness of the man.

"You too, Sir Henry, do you understand?"

I nodded, as much at the spite in which he'd said my name as in agreement to his terms. I smiled to myself. Having been trumped by Sir Thomas Lynch, he now had the further indignity of sharing his title with the nephew of one of his lieutenants.

Tarr nudged me and I realized my smile had grown and was showing on my face.

"Captain," he said. Morgan raised an eyebrow and my uncle quickly amended his title. "Sir Henry, what of the crews? How many men does *Freyja* have?"

"Thirty, hale and hearty," Hornigold answered for Morgan, with a self-satisfied smirk. Whether at the number of men under his command, or the rhyme he had made was known only to him.

"She'll need more to fight well. Sharpe here will join you." I started and looked at Tarr in surprise. "You'll take Jonesy and Little as well. Any ideas, Blake?"

"Cheval."

"Oh yes, Cheval. We'll find you a half dozen more in addition."

My heart sank. Of all the men to sail with, I had to endure the company of the sycophantic Frenchman as well as the "evil little bastard". So much for my new life running a sugar plantation.

"Excellent." Morgan downed another glass of rum and slammed it onto the table with a loud crack. Shards of glass fountained over his hand to the table and floor.

"*Damn it*," Morgan shouted. "Damn fool bloody things! He wiped blood from the back of his hand. "It's been a long time since anyone's bloodied me, van Ecken, the last one lost his guts and danced around them."

The van Eckens blanched.

"Luckily for ye, knights of the realm don't indulge in such activities, but that won't stop me if it happens again. Ye'll serve me with a tankard on my next visit."

The elder van Ecken opened his mouth, but Morgan waved him to silence. "We'll take our leave. Hornigold, where's my coat?"

Erik stuck his head through the dining room door and shouted for Hendrick, who soon appeared with a selection of gaily colored frockcoats, and Tarr took the opportunity to whisper in my ear.

"Keep an eye on him, Henry. I need someone I can trust on that boat. You're my eyes and ears."

I was handed my coat before I could respond.

Chapter 16

I, along with every other man aboard *Freyja* and, no doubt, *Edelweiss*, held my breath as we glided past the huge fort of San Felipe de Todo Fierro. Phil's Iron Fort as Tarr insisted on calling it.

We had waited for a moonless night and a gentle breeze. The sails, after being coated with the blackest of tar, were set and would not be adjusted until we were past the fort; we could not afford any creaking lines or flapping canvas. There was no noise and little to see in the dark of night. Soon, the glimmers of lantern light that marked the fort were at our stern, then in our wake. Another five minutes and a bend in the river, and the fort was gone. As one, the men on *Freyja's* deck heaved a sigh of relief to have made it past the huge rectangular structure, laden with iron, but we had bigger challenges ahead.

Porto Belo was guarded by two more forts—two! Santiago de la Gloria—Santiago's Glory—and San Jerónimo. Together they bristled with over a score of guns and boasted over a hundred men to fire them.

"I hope your uncle knows what he's doing," Jonesy whispered.

"So do I," I replied.

"Don't fret, boys," Little stepped in, "Tarr and Blake were here with Morgan back in '68. They know the town and its defenses well."

"A lot can change in fifteen years," Jonesy said.

"Four or five years ago, everything was the same, just not as heavily guarded," Little said.

"How do you know?" I asked.

"Coxton raided it in '78, La Sonda the year after. Apparently the captain knows them both well." Little nodded toward Hornigold.

"Why not as heavily guarded?" I asked. "If they've been raided so often why haven't they employed more guards?"

"They have, but there are only so many men—the extra men all sail with the treasure fleet itself. With any luck we'll have our pick of the treasures before the fleet gets here."

The treasure fleet—near a score of galleons packed to the gunwales with gold, silver and jewels —sailed for Spain most years in March and September. Porto Belo was one of the stops of the Armada de Tierra Firme to load up; mainly with silver from the enormous mine that was Potosi—a mountain literally of silver—but also with gold and jewels from Peru. They would spend over a month here loading up before journeying on to Cartagena and other treasure-rich ports, then Havana to meet up with the second fleet; the Fleet of New Spain, before embarking for Old Spain.

"Lights ahead," an urgent whisper was thrust back along the deck to Hornigold.

"Helm a lee," he responded, putting as much urgency into his hoarse whisper as possible. "Put her head to wind and bring the canoe alongside. Sharpshooters, get your muskets."

With a sigh, Jonesy, Little and I bent to pick up our loads. Muskets, ball, powder and plenty of match. I checked my pockets for my steel and flint, then passed the bundles down to the men stowing them.

When everything was safely aboard, the three of us, plus half a dozen more, clambered into the long canoe and cast off.

Tarr's canoe, similarly filled, came alongside and we paddled eastward. We needed to sneak up to Santiago's Glory's beach, and trek up the hill to our positions. It was going to be a long night.

Chapter 17

The sky had lightened enough for us all to see each other, and it wouldn't be long before the sun broke the horizon.

We had reached the hill without incident and were near the top when Cheval whispered, "Down!"

I immediately fell to my belly, as did the others. "There's a sentry up there, they must 'ave posted him after Morgan used these 'ills last time." Cheval sounded worried.

I lifted my head, then rose to my knees to have a proper look. A single-story stone building perched on top of the hill. A man's head appeared above the castellations of its roof. I waited a while, but could not see anyone else. I fumbled to untie one of the muskets from my bundle, loaded it, and crept a little further up the slope.

"What are you doing? You'll never 'it 'im at this range!" Cheval hissed. I ignored him, took aim and fired. The man fell and my crewmates cheered.

I met Cheval's eyes. He looked furious. I raised my eyebrows at him but he stayed silent.

"Come on, let's go, Tarr will have taken that shot as the signal, we need to get into position quickly."

Cheval said, "Wait . . ." but everyone ignored him and twenty men stormed up the final incline. Jonesy and I were the first to reach the stone building and we ran inside. Nobody there, just a table, chair and cot. Basic accommodations for one.

Back outside, Cheval was arguing again; this time over shooting positions. He wanted the prime spot on the roof.

"You can't shoot for shit, Cheval," Little said.

Cheval made to protest, but was stayed by everybody else's agreement. "Sharpe and Jonesy take the roof, you're the two most likely to hit anything," he said instead. "The rest of you, spread out." His voice rose to a shout as he pointed out to sea.

I squinted and spotted sail approaching through the early morning mist.

"They'll be in range soon. We have to be ready." He grabbed his muskets and lay on the slope above Santiago, as did the rest of the men.

I ran up the outside steps to the roof of the hut, closely followed by Jonesy and one of the boys, Billy Mac, who would reload for us. Dropping the muskets, I grabbed the dead soldier's shoulders, and Jonesy his feet, then we heaved him over the wall.

Turning back to seaward, I saw the boy had already untied both bundles of muskets and he handed a loaded one to me, then another to Jonesy. The two of us found our positions, standing and bracing on one of the crenelations, and stared down at the view.

The sun broke free and the first rays danced over turquoise water, lush green slopes, and enormous stone forts bristling with ironwork.

San Jerónimo was across the harbor mouth. A copy of Phil's Iron Fort, its longest side presented to the harbor with near a dozen great guns aimed at the water, and our vessels. It was well out of range of our muskets; Tarr and Hornigold would have to work hard to best it. But

Santiago's Glory, nestled on another hill below, was ours to suppress.

It was enormous, with a pitched roof in the middle of its quad, housing who knew how many men. I counted seven guns and scores of men rushing to them. My shot had raised the alarm.

I waited, as did the rest of us. Billy loaded the last muskets and I nodded my thanks at him. *Edelweiss* and *Freyja* glided closer. The mist was burning off quickly, and surely the Spaniards would spot their dull sails soon. Even as I thought the words, one of Jerónimo's great guns exploded, and both ships immediately retaliated, deadly iron ball flying back and forth.

The fort below us exploded into action. Men, still half-dressed, at the laborious task of preparing their first volley. I focused on the officer bellowing orders and waving his arms. The musket was heavy in my hands and I used the weight rather than fighting it to find the right balance. I shifted my feet a little. That was better.

I aimed carefully for his gut. The guns were far from accurate, and aiming there would give me the best chance of hitting the man. I took a deep breath, let it out. Breathed in again, then out. A third breath, then a squeeze of the trigger as I exhaled. I blinked, my calm shattered by the noise of the musket firing, then grinned in satisfaction at the sight of my quarry dropping, his head a bloody mess. I handed the empty gun to Billy and picked up another full one. My crewmates opened fire and panic reigned Santiago; Spanish soldiers dived for cover, leaving their canon unattended.

I squeezed the trigger and another man fell. Exchanged guns. Fired. On and on until the only soldiers still in view on Santiago's battlements were either dead or dying. Tarr and the others would have no problems from this shore.

Chapter 18

The battle across the harbor mouth was in full force. Fountains of water sprayed when balls missed the attacking ships, but enough hit their targets to make life difficult for Tarr and Hornigold.

I fell to the floor in a tangle of limbs with Jonesy and Billy. Deafened, I pushed myself to my feet and peeped over the battlements of our miniature tower. San Jerónimo was a smoking ruin. The shore party, putting off under the bellow of cannon, had successfully landed and infiltrated the huge building whilst its men had been preoccupied with the two ships. They'd only had one objective—to find the armory and blow up the powder magazine within it. By the looks of things it had been well-stocked.

The Edelweissers and Freyjamen had their longboats halfway back to the ships. Next, it was the turn of Santiago's Glory to be demolished.

A great gun fired from below us. "What's that?" Jonesy cried. "Where is it?"

"I can't see! It must be lower down, out of sight of this place. *Come on*. Bring the guns, Billy!"

We raced down the steps and re-joined our crewmates.

"The gun's positioned so we can't see it from here,

Jonesy and I will go and see if we can silence it." I pointed down the hill. We would have to skirt the castle and come up on its flank.

"*No.* You stay 'ere, keep these guns silenced, I'll go with Little."

I couldn't argue, Cheval was my quartermaster. I glanced at Jonesy and he met my eye; we both knew his motivation, and it wasn't to save the two ships still under fire. He wanted glory; and to prevent us from obtaining any more.

A gun from the ramparts fired, and I ran up the steps again. Tarr and the others didn't have time for me to argue with Cheval.

I fired, again hitting my mark; the guns placed in the battlements were silent once more, their remaining men fleeing back to safety. Cheval and half a dozen others ran downhill and were soon out of sight. I could only hope Cheval's bravery matched his cunning. *Edelweiss* and *Freyja* bombarded the castle walls, and I saw ball still issuing from the castle and winced as one hit the water close enough for the spray to soak the men on deck. They were too close! If the ships went down we were all dead.

A cheer behind me startled me; my hearing was returning. I turned to glare at Billy, then looked to where he was pointing. A stream of men was running across the hillside, away from the fort, chased by Cheval and his group. They were fleeing! They'd abandoned their castle.

"*They're running.*" Billy was dancing a jig now." Yellow-bellied, lily-livered scum!"

I glanced at Jonesy and smiled in relief. We knew it had been a possibility; they'd run when Morgan had attacked and, by the looks of things, there were even fewer men stationed here today than there had been then.

"It seems the men of New Spain are not of the same

determined breed as their brethren of Old," Jonesy smirked.

The longboats landed to no resistance and privateers stormed the castle. Grappling hooks attached to long lines provided easy access to men who had been swarming rigging most of their lives.

"Come on, we done here," I said to Jonesy and Billy. We regathered the muskets, all reloaded now, thanks to Billy's nimble fingers, and headed back down to join the others.

By the time we reached the longboats, there was a steady stream of men returning and clutching prizes: pistols; a Spanish rapier; a tortoiseshell box; a decorative frockcoat. Cheval and his group were with them; they hadn't bothered with the chase for long.

We clambered in and pushed off.

Mighty shoulders, developed through years of hauling hemp and canon, powered the boats through the choppy water and we were back aboard our motherships in moments.

Hornigold grasped Cheval's hand. "Well done, mate. That was some shooting up there, you cleared them out faster than rats leaving a sinking prize!"

Cheval grinned in pleasure, but the men glanced uneasily at each other, then at Jonesy and me. I stayed quiet, knowing the men knew who had the sharp eyes and steady trigger fingers. The captain could be voted out; the crew were the important ones on this ship.

"*Full sail,*" Hornigold shouted. "*Porto Belo ahoy.*"

The crew cheered and the topmen swarmed to the topyards, forty feet above the deck. Swathes of canvas fell and were hauled in until they bellied with wind. Speed was important now, not stealth.

We held our breath—and our great guns at the ready—as we approached the town.

Chapter 19

The mist had cleared, but sulfurous gun smoke hung over the sheltered harbor, wisping against the sails. Our speed slowed as we approached, the high land sheltering our lower courses from the wind and they flapped as the topsail did its best to drive us forward.

I was on the maintop with Jonesy, a dozen muskets tied loosely to the mast to prevent them falling, my wig jammed tightly to my head. Our sharpshooting duties had not yet resumed though; for the moment we were simply lookouts.

Jerónimo was still ablaze; its smoke our companion on our slow drift toward Porto Belo. I glanced at Jonesy, his eyes were red raw and streaming and I blinked and wiped my own to peer through the shifting, stinking tendrils.

A shape became more distinct as we neared. I squinted; large and rectangular, it could only be one thing.

"*Gun battery off our larboard bow,*" I cried loudly enough for the men on deck to hear.

"Ready your guns," Hornigold ordered in response.

I glanced over at *Edelweiss*, just behind and to larboard. As the wind had lightened, the larger, heavier ship had slowed and the light, maneuverable *Freyja* had crept ahead to lead the way.

I jumped as the sound of a cannon reverberated around the harbor and the hills surrounding it. The battery may be small, but it was armed and manned.

Edelweiss swung slowly to starboard, presenting her broadside to the stone rampart, and *Freyja* followed suit.

We both flung broadside after broadside at them; upwards of twenty ball every three minutes from the two vessels.

Their return fire was sporadic and I realized they only had men for three or four guns. I thought back; those Spaniards hadn't fled Santiago's Glory, they'd retreated here. And Cheval had let them run!

I glanced down at the deck and spotted him at Hornigold's right hand, strutting around the quarterdeck with his captain, relaying orders to the gunners. I was tempted to pick up one of the muskets and shoot him myself. Jonesy stayed my hand before I even realized I'd reached out for a weapon.

"Not worth it, Sharpe mate, you'd only end up hanged or worse."

I glanced up at him in surprise. He raised his eyebrows and I realized my thoughts had been clear on my face. I'd have to take more care over that.

Freyja rolled under the force of another broadside and we both grabbed the mast and each other to steady ourselves. The maintop was a four-by-four-foot wooden platform at the height of the mainyard; thirty feet above deck, and precarious at the best of times, never mind in the midst of a gun battle.

"If he'd chased down those Spaniards, or let us go after them, those guns would be silent," I told Jonesy angrily.

"You don't know that; men from the town itself could be manning them."

"The fat, rich merchants? Has the sun addled your wits? They wouldn't have the strength to bring one of those guns to bear."

Jonesy shrugged and I sighed in exasperation. He was right. It didn't matter who was loading and setting a match to them, we could do nothing about it now bar fight back.

"We're drifting closer, let's see if we can pick some of these buggers off," Jonesy said, handing me a loaded musket.

I steadied myself against the mast, swayed with *Freyja's* motion over the waves, and paid attention to the rhythm of the gunners below. *Freyja's* reaction to their powder going off was more than enough to disturb my aim.

A broadside exploded and Freyja heeled to starboard. I pressed against the mast, waiting for her to level out and settle. I kept my eye trained on my mark, a man in red and white standing behind the closest cannon wedged into the small castellation. I squeezed my trigger, but missed. The range was still too great. Then he fell as another musket fired and Jonesy cheered. "*Hah.* I beat you to a shot, mate! What's wrong, your hands atremble?"

I turned to face him, his hands aloft holding the musket like a trophy. "Lucky sh—" I broke off as another broadside fired below us.

Jonesy's face turned from elation to terror. He dropped the musket, arms waving to find some purchase. I grabbed the mast with one hand and lunged, but was too late. My grasping fingers found only air.

Jonesy's scream was cut off by a thump and I stared down at his broken body on the deck below. Hornigold and Cheval rushed to him and bent over him, then straightened and looked up at me. He was dead.

I squinted. *Is Cheval grinning?*

I rubbed my eyes of smoke, but he had turned away and I could no longer see his face.

I glanced up at a cheer from *Edelweiss* and noticed her jibs in tatters and her bowsprit missing, then I turned my gaze to the gun battery and saw the reason for their elation. It had crumbled. Porto Belo and her treasures were defenseless.

Chapter 20

The guns silenced and a hush filled the air along with more gun smoke. I slowly made my way down the ratlins, terrified of what I'd find on deck.

A circle of men had formed around Jonesy and I pushed my way through as Hornigold shouted for the boats to be launched. I knelt in a vacated space and lifted Jonesy's head, then dropped it in recoil at the grinding, squelching noise my action had produced. He would not draw breath again.

"*Sharpe*," a voice shouted loudly enough to raise me from my contemplation of my friend's visage. "To the boats. Quick, man!"

"Oh leave 'im, Capitaine, 'e's no use to man nor beast shedding tears over 'is mate. Leave 'im to keep ship," Cheval called. "Look at 'im, you'd think 'im a spinster who'd lost 'er last chance at an 'usband!" He laughed and a couple of his cronies joined in, then the deck cleared and I was alone with Jonesy.

"I'm so sorry, my friend, so sorry," I whispered, stroking his hair away from his face. "You joined me to find new life, only to find death."

I stayed, kneeling in his blood for some time, then rose and made my way below decks. I pulled at the securing lines of his Brazilian bed and the canvas fell to the deck. I gathered it up and made my way to the closest sail locker for needle and twine, then hefted my load back up the ladder to the topdeck.

I laid the canvas out alongside Jonesy and carefully, painstakingly, shifted his body across until he lay on his bed, careful to straighten his legs, his arms, his neck. Next, I placed a 6lb ball at his feet for ballast then sewed the edges of his shroud together, enclosing him in canvas; up to his knees, thighs, belly.

"Damn and blast," I exclaimed, the sound of my own voice startling me as I jabbed the thick needle into the pad of my thumb. Blood, mixed with tears I'd been unaware of, dripped onto the canvas and I continued to sew.

I tugged the canvas hard to wrap it around his shoulders, the two edges only just meeting, and secured it tightly. Now only his face was visible: pale, with bloodstains creeping across his skin. I stared at him a minute; two; five; then folded the bloody canvas over and finished my task. My hands, arms and knees were soaked in blood; both mine and his. I knotted the twine for the final time, cut it and whispered a final prayer over his corpse. "Sleep well, my friend, sleep well."

Chapter 21

An explosion from the shore dragged my attention away from my shrouded mate and I made my way forward. I squinted toward the town and held my breath against the stink of the exposed mud a couple of hundred yards ahead. Hours had passed whilst I'd knelt over Jonesy and the tide was going out quickly; my shipmates would have to hurry or we'd be stranded here until the next tide's flood.

I glanced across at *Edelweiss*; with her deeper draught she was anchored further out, but I didn't know how far the tide ebbed here. I was pleased to see they had rigged up a replacement bowsprit—no doubt a spare mainyard— she'd be able to make sail at least.

Another gunshot echoed from the town and I turned my attention landward again. At least half the seafront warehouses were ablaze. I could see no Spaniards, only privateers firing into the air, dragging chests, clutching leather bags full of booty, and whooping and hollering as they brought Hell to Porto Belo in their quest for gold.

I loaded one of the 2lb rail guns and fired to catch the attention of the sailors. Gold, Spanish brandy, and no doubt Spanish women had taken their minds and hearts far from any shipboard concerns. They needed reminding. We had no idea if any of the Spanish soldiers had gone for reinforcements; we could not tarry and be caught here till the next tide with no means of escape.

After a second shot from the rail gun, I saw the men drift toward the boats and I stood unmoved—no pity, no horror, no delight—and waited for the boats to return. I turned my attention back to Jonesy. Soon the decks would be heaving with gold-rich, besotted privateers. This would be my last chance to pay quiet respects to my fallen friend.

I got back to my feet as the first boat arrived at the ship. Hornigold was first aboard, followed by a young woman. *No, still a girl*, I thought.

"The customs house was empty. *Goddammit*. That's Tarr for you—always bloody tardy. But there were plenty of spoils if you knew where to look, and I've found a beauty!" He dragged the girl closer to him and she cringed away, although kept her composure I noted, impressed. Young with long, dark, curly hair, piercing eyes and a defiant cast to the set of her jaw, she reminded me a little of Erik van Ecken's new wife, Gabriella, but I pushed those thoughts out of mind. I could not, would not, think of her. I had met her two months before, just after meeting Morgan. *Freyja* had been dispatched to Massachusetts Bay to bring her to Sayba and her marriage. She'd had a spirit I'd admired on that passage, and had managed to hold onto it despite her wedding. I doubted it would last much longer.

"Oui, plenty of gold too," Cheval chimed in. "The treasure fleet may 'ave sailed, but they spent a lot of coin 'ere first!" He held up a heavy pouch, bulging no doubt with silver rather than the gold he claimed.

"Ah. What do we have here?" He crossed to Jonesy's

body. "So you've been paying respects to the dead while we've been at work making profit? Where's the sense in that? You fool, 'e's gone, 'e can't 'elp you now." He kicked Jonesy and I leapt at him, but was stilled by screams. The girl. She was staring at the bloody shroud, then at me, still screaming. I looked down at myself. I was covered in blood and saw myself as she no doubt did: a murderous devil, my attire reflecting the color of the flag at our masthead.

I held out my hand in a placating gesture, but Hornigold shook her and threw her to the deck. "Blast thee, girl! Avast that infernal noise."

She stopped and Hornigold grinned in relief. He clearly hadn't seen the fire in her eyes, the hate that burned there as she regarded him.

I pulled myself up to my full height, squared my shoulders, and glared at my captain, thankful that I wore my wig for any battle or foray ashore. It reminded me of my old life, the man I had been—Lord Rowleston, the Earl of Shirehampton—and brought me the authority my title and position bestowed, even aboard a privateer vessel.

His gaze flickered under my stare and I knew that was my cue. "What are you doing with her?"

"Whatever I like and it's none of your damn concern, Sharpe!"

I raised my eyebrows and paused before I spoke. "Anything that occurs aboard this boat is Tarr's concern, and as his agent and nephew, it is therefore mine. No women aboard *Edelweiss* or *Freyja*, it's in the articles you signed, as you know well."

"*Bah.* Hellfire on the articles, she's a spoil of war. Anyway, she won't be aboard long, just time enough for us all to enjoy her, then she's shark food!"

A handful of men cheered at this and I stared at them,

noting who had given their approval to this course of action. Cheval, of course, Prince, Savage and half a dozen others. I glared at them each in turn and they quietened.

"We are under license from King Charles, we do nothing to dishonor his name, nor will I allow you to sully the reputation of my uncle!"

"Well, we're under Morgan's license, anyroad." Hornigold laughed and I narrowed my eyes at him, but I let the comment pass. I glanced down at the girl, she was my concern now; if I did not save her, I would truly become the devil she thought I was.

"Put her ashore, Hornigold."

"No. Who the blazes do you think you are to give me, the *captain*, orders?"

"Lord Rowleston-Sharpe, nephew of your commander. I take my orders from him, not you," I sneered. "And you'd do well to take heed."

Hornigold opened his mouth, but nothing came out. The deck was shrouded in silence as the Freyjamen waited to see who would win this battle of wills. Even the girl was silent, glancing between myself and Hornigold from her position on the deck.

Freyja lurched slightly and a shout rose up, "*Captain.* The tide! If we don't go now we'll be stuck in this infernal, stinking mud."

"*Slip the anchor,*" Hornigold shouted, but not before I saw a flash of relief pass over his eyes. "Set the jibs and topsail, get us away from this hellhole!"

Men ran to do his bidding, Little giving me a nod as he passed, blade drawn to cut the anchor line. More ran to mast and sheet to set sail, while others pushed us out to sea on the next wave with long boathooks. Sinking into the mud with every thrust, they were of little more use than none, but we needed every inch to escape.

I glanced over to *Edelweiss*, worried about her larger hull, but she was already free of her anchor and setting sail. I furrowed my brow, wondering why she was towing the one ship we hadn't sunk in this harbor, then transferred my attention back to Hornigold.

He turned back to me in triumph. "No one's going ashore now, Sharpe, you can show her to my cabin to wait until I'm ready for her."

"No."

He stared at me, but I could sense he was intimidated. I had not forgotten that flash of relief when we'd been interrupted earlier, and knew he was terrified of Uncle Richard, however much bravado he showed in his presence. He could not punish me in the way he would any other member of his crew; Tarr would have him keelhauled, and he knew it. Tarr had been very clear that I was aboard as his agent, to ensure obedience to the commander of our little fleet. The only recourse Hornigold had was to challenge me to a duel, but he knew well, as did every other man aboard, that he was no match for my skill with blade or pistol.

He glanced around. Every man was busy, no one had heard my refusal except himself and Cheval. I stared at the Frenchman; he would feel my ire soon. I would not let his kick to Jonesy go unpunished, but for now I had to protect the living.

"She stays with me and we will take the second cabin."

Hornigold smirked and the girl stared at me in disgust.

"No man, including myself, will touch you unless you permit it," I told her. She stared at me a moment, then nodded. I turned my attention back to Hornigold. "Any man touches her, I will gut him, do you understand?"

He moved his head; barely perceptible, but it was a nod nonetheless.

"But that's *my* cabin," Cheval whined.

"Not anymore, Quartermaster, we have a guest," Hornigold said without looking at him.

I nodded to the captain and held my hand out to the girl. She hesitated, then took it and allowed me to help her to her feet. I offered her my arm, which she also took, then I led her aft to the hatch and the cabins below.

"Get that lump of meat off my decks."

My step faltered at Hornigold's command, but I didn't stop. I had already spoken the appropriate words over Jonesy, paid my respects, and said my goodbyes.

"What's your name, girl?" I asked as a distant part of me registered the splash of Jonesy's journey to his final resting place.

"Magdalena."

Chapter 22

I ushered Magdalena into the cabin and told her to make herself comfortable.

"What do wi' me?" She stood tall, chin jutting out, fire in her eyes, despite her broken English.

"Calm yourself, no harm will come to you whilst you are under my protection."

"What will . . . *protection*," she spat the word at me, "cost? What price?"

I shook my head with a rueful smile. "Did you not hear me out on deck?" I nodded toward the cabin door. "No man aboard this vessel, including myself, will touch you without your permission. Allow it," I amended at her blank look.

"You think I'll give *you* allow?" She was bolder now it was only the two of us and I smiled in appreciation of her strong spirit.

"I haven't asked for it," I said mildly.

Her mouth opened, then closed as she found no rejoinder.

"Sit down, we have a long voyage ahead, you may as well make yourself comfortable."

"I prefer stand," she said, then staggered as *Freyja* picked up speed and heeled. We were leaving the harbor for the less sheltered River Chagres. "Where going?"

"Sayba," I replied, "in the Northern Antilles."

"And what there?"

I sighed and sat on the cot. "I don't yet know. My uncle captains the other ship you saw, I will transfer us both there at the first opportunity so Captain Hornigold cannot cause us harm. Then I'll find a way to get you home."

"I don't want," she said, finally sitting on the chair by the chart table. "No Porto Belo."

I raised my eyebrows. "Why ever not?"

She sighed. "Is long story."

"As I said, long voyage ahead."

She looked at me a moment, then her shoulders slumped. She was badly in need of a friend, and had just come to the realization herself. My heart went out to her, this lost soul, and in that instant she reminded me of myself before Jonesy had found me and rescued me from my folly. My vision clouded as I thought of him. His salvation of me had led to his own death, and I vowed I would honor his memory any way I could; by living well myself, and making sure this slip of a girl came to no harm.

"Your story?" I prompted, anxious to drag myself away from thoughts of Jonesy.

She stared at her hands, then looked up at me. "I waited Leo. I thought your sail his, then saw two and heard guns. I knew. No Leo."

"Who's Leo?"

"Friend. I know him long time, we survive Panama."

"Morgan's attack?"

She nodded. "His papá y mamá dead. Mi familia bring

him Porto Belo. We hate. The stink, the way town go mad with treasure fever then dies, ever year. I die ever year too."

I nodded, I could imagine all the hustle and excitement, then . . . nothing.

"When Leo old, he work for mi papá, sailing. His next sail, he captain, and I be wife, stuck in hellhole, bebés hanging off skirts, dying ever year. No. No live that. So when piratas come—"

"Privateers," I corrected.

"—I no run."

"Do you realize what would have happened to you had I not been aboard?"

She shrugged. "I no think. I just . . . run. I want escape, Aventura. You both."

"Come here," I said, and led her to the gallery of windows. I threw them open and we stood in the fresh air on the small railed ledge over the sea.

"There. That's what we have to offer." I pointed at the remains of Santiago's Glory and San Jerónimo. "Destruction and death. That's what these men offer. Yes, there may be adventure, but who will it turn you into?"

Chapter 23

When I walked back out onto deck, dusk was already falling and I recognized the shape of the headland ahead. San Felipe de Todo Fierro was not far away.

"Leave your fancy woman be, Sharpe," Cheval snapped, and I glared at him. He ignored my stare. "You're needed in the tops, Little's already there. Look sharp, Sharpe." He laughed at his own joke and I headed for the main ratlins to begin my climb. Cheval could wait; for now.

The mainsail flogged loudly and I flinched. It was strange to climb past the tarred sails, they were all but invisible in the gloom; ghostly wraiths of sail. Last time, they had brought us safely past the heavily defended fort unseen, but these men would know of our attack on Porto Belo; they would not be dozing at their guns tonight.

I greeted Little as I swung myself onto the maintop platform and picked up a musket.

"All loaded?" I inquired.

"Aye, ready and willing," came the reply.

I said no more and settled down to await the first shooting opportunity.

I could only make out Tarr's ship ahead by the eerie

white glow of her wake and remembered the ship he had towed out of Porto Belo harbor.

"You'll see," Little said with a chuckle when I mentioned it. "He's a wily old bastard, your uncle, don't do anything without good reason, him."

I pursed my lips and decided it was a compliment, then shifted position to get as comfortable as possible.

With no lights showing, blackened sails, and the crew below working in near silence, there was scarce anything to see or hear. It felt as if Little and I were floating along on one of the Moorish magic carpets I'd heard tell of in stories. Forty feet above the sea; blackness above and darkness below. Then a spark flared ahead and burst into flame.

"What the blazes?" I exclaimed, jumping to my feet and grabbing the mast to peer closely at the phenomenon.

"Hah. Wily old bastard, told you," Little said. "Get your gun ready. With any luck, their night sight will be killed by the fireship and it'll draw all their ball, but you never know."

I realized the fireball was the ship Uncle Richard had towed and as it drifted downriver on the tide, it was being pulled closer and closer to the fort.

I squinted and just made out the *Edelweiss* as she bore away toward the shore opposite the fort, and felt *Freyja* cant as she changed course to follow.

Cannon fired from the fort and a cheer below was quickly hushed by Hornigold. The ruse had worked, they were firing on the decoy.

I joined Little in mumbling a small, although slightly blasphemous, prayer and kept my eyes on the fort. Little breathed a sigh of relief. "All clear, we're past."

A shout off our larboard bow caught my attention and I

peered into the night. *Is Edelweiss in trouble?*

"Little! What's happening?"

He stopped laughing and squinted toward our sister ship. "Oh bugger, she's aground." He dropped his musket, grabbed hold of the backstay and slid down the fifty-foot stretch of hemp to the deck below. I winced; the skin on his hands must be thicker than leather.

I heard him talk to Hornigold, then our course adjusted back to the middle of the river. "What? No!"

I took a deep breath, then jumped and caught hold of the backstay as I'd seen Little do, and screamed in pain all the way down to the deck, my hands burning from the rope. I let go a little too early, unable to grip it any longer and fell in a heap, much to Hornigold's amusement.

"What are you doing? We've got to help them."

"Ahh, he's only touched bottom, he'll get the boats out, haul himself off and be out of the Chagres in no time."

"You don't know that. His jib is jury-rigged. Go back, *Freyja* can haul him free."

"We're in the dammed river, Sharpe. There's no room to tack or wear round. Tarr knows it even if you don't, blasted land-crab that you are. *Edelweiss* is on her own, just as *Freyja* would be had it been the other way round. Now get back up that blasted mast and stay there, we're sailing blind, I need my sharpest eyes in the tops, and unfortunately that means you."

Chapter 24

"You're no use to sailor nor ship," Prince said as he joined me on the maintop. "You're supposed to be keeping a lookout ahead not astern. Captain's sent me to relieve you. That woman's whipping up a storm in t' cabin, you've to set her to rights."

"*Edelweiss* is free of the shore," I told him. "But she must be damaged, she's slow."

"Tarr'll be right. He'll bring ship and crew home safe, don't fret."

I glanced at him with a smile, then remembered the rest of his message. "What's Magdalena doing?"

"Dunno, mate, but it don't sound good. Best get in there before Captain or Quartermaster beat you to it."

"Aye, ta, mate." My elocution was definitely heading south, and at rapid speed. I glanced at the backstay and grimaced, then noticed Cheval was not on deck. I leaped for the stay and slid, my hands red raw. I jumped through the hatch to the deck below, tucking my poor hands under my armpits, but it didn't help.

Making my way aft, I found Little lounging on a barrel before the cabin door. "Little," I said, wary, "what are you doing?"

"Oh, Sharpe, thank the Christ, I didn't know what to do." He thumped the wooden wall and shouted. I looked at him in puzzlement, then opened the door.

Cheval had hold of Magdalena's wrist. It looked like she'd just slapped him. He turned. "Little! I told you to make sure no one—" He broke off when he saw me.

"My apologies, Quartermaster, I tried, but he overpowered me," Little said, holding his jaw. Now I understood why he had hit the wall. He glanced at me and dipped his head, urging me toward Cheval and Magdalena.

"Let go of her."

Cheval sneered. "Make me."

Magdalena suddenly thrust her knee upwards, catching Cheval between the legs, and wrenched her arm free.

I stared at her in surprise as Cheval grunted and doubled over in pain. Behind me, Little stifled a laugh and Cheval glared at me. "I'll teach you to laugh at me, Sharpe, I'll teach you!"

He pushed past us and made his way out of the cabin. Little met my eye, looking worried. I held up my hand to forestall his apology.

"No need to fret, Little. He's already gunning for me, there's little sense in both of us having him for an enemy." I tilted my head toward the door and he nodded, then made his way out. I turned back to Magdalena.

"Did he hurt you?"

"No, I didn't allow."

I wanted to reprimand her, I'd had enough problems with Cheval and Hornigold before having this woman aboard under my protection, I didn't need her making things worse, but I couldn't help the twitch of my lips.

Her own twitched in response and I burst out laughing so hard I was bent almost double and had to prop myself up on my knees. All the emotion of the past few days flooded out of me as tears streamed down my face: the tension of the raid, the men I had killed, Jonesy's death, Uncle Richard aground, and my public disagreements with Cheval and Hornigold.

Eventually my guffaws died down and I wiped my eyes. Magdalena's merriment had subsided long before my own and she was looking at me strangely.

"My apologies, señorita, it has been an eventful two days."

"Aventura?"

"Aye, you could say that." I looked up at her and the smile on her face, and my heart plummeted. This was only the start.

PART THREE

February 1684

Chapter 25

Tarr and *Edelweiss* had caught up with us at Sayba, and I had never been so relieved to see somebody in my life. He was all I had; my only family and my closest friend. Little and Prince had proved to be worthwhile acquaintances, but I wouldn't call either of them a true friend, neither of them could rival Jonesy. And then there was Magdalena. Ah, Magdalena, what to say of her? Headstrong, beautiful, infuriating, strong-willed, beautiful, beautiful, beautiful. I spent almost every minute I was not on watch, with her; I had kept her safe aboard *Freyja*, yet she never let me touch her apart from the odd, supplicating kiss of her hand.

Tarr had been furious and had wanted to leave her ashore in Sayba. She may have been good company for Gabriella van Ecken, but I could not imagine her presence in that house bringing anything other than hardship for both women. Besides, I was becoming enamored of her. I could not be in Gabriella's life or make things right for her, but I could for Magdalena.

After a few months, Magdalena remaining at my side, Tarr had relented, and I transferred to *Edelweiss* with my prize, leaving the powder keg of jealousy and resentment that *Freyja* had become.

As soon as I'd vacated Hornigold's decks, he'd disappeared. He'd been off our larboard quarter at dusk, and was nowhere to be seen come dawn. Tarr was furious.

"*Sail oh.*" My eyes had spotted the prize to the west: a three-master with beautiful lines and a hull low in the water, laden with cargo.

Tarr held his glass to his eye and beckoned me to join him on deck. I grabbed the backstay and slid down; my palms now as tough as old leather.

"She's a beauty," my uncle said. "I reckon it's time to trade up, we could do with more room aboard now the crew numbers over a hundred, and it'll put that bugger Hornigold in his place when he shows his face again. "*All hands on deck,*" he added at a roar, taking me by surprise. "Ready the guns, prepare for battle!"

Edelweiss's decks heaved with purpose as cannon were readied, powder and shot brought up, and a preparatory round of rum downed. Little and I carried *Edelweiss's* collection of muskets topside, loaded them and stacked them butt down in a couple of barrels which we then swayed to the tops. I followed the guns to the maintop and helped Little secure them to the mast. I also had large pouches of powder, ball and wadding in case we needed to reload.

I glanced down and watched my crewmates clear everything bar weapon and line from the decks, then cursed. Magdalena, dressed in a pair of my breeches and shirt appeared on deck.

"That bleedin' woman!" Little spluttered. "What in the name of Hell does she think she's doing?"

I sighed, noticed Tarr make his way over to her, and slid

down to the deck for the second time in less than an hour.

"—bloody skirt on my deck in battle!" Tarr's face was cochineal red as he roared at Magdalena. She looked down at herself then back up at Tarr.

"I see no skirt, Capitán, only willing hands and sharp eye."

I landed beside them, grabbed Magdalena and pulled her off to the main hatch before Tarr could retaliate. He looked to be ready to use his fists; or a blade.

"What the blazes do you think you're doing? You're barely tolerated at the best of times aboard this ship, did you really think you'd be welcomed in a battle?"

"*No*. That's lie!"

"Is it?"

"Sí. I most welcome from crew."

I laughed. "Only the ones who want to explore beneath your skirts."

She thrust her hands on her hips and pushed her face up toward mine. "*Mierda*. That's all bloody men think, sí? What under skirt. And I know all *you* blasted well think."

I held up my hands in defense, shocked at her command of the vulgarities of the English language. "Watch your mouth, señorita, I've never laid a hand on you, *or* tried to lift your skirts!"

"No, but you want, why else you keep me?"

I opened my mouth, but no words were ready. Magdalena raised her eyebrows in a smirk. "Play your game, or your . . . dice, right, and you may get."

I reddened with embarrassment. "Have you no shame?"

"Shame? Me? No. But steady hands and sharp eyes. I no leave Porto Belo to be hide and lock in cabin."

I raised my own eyebrows. "You did not choose to leave Porto Belo, señorita, you were taken."

"Sí?"

I looked away from her frank gaze, unsure what to believe. After eight months of her stubborn, wilful, *infuriating* company, I still did not know what to believe of her. My breath grew heavy as I regarded her, and her look turned triumphant.

"Go to the cabin. When the fight begins, no one will have a mind as to your whereabouts. But stay on this ship and I want no complaints if you're hurt."

She smiled, rose up to her toes, caressed my cheek with her hand, and planted a small kiss on my lips, then turned and clambered through the hatch and out of sight.

I sighed and raised my fingers to my lips. I would have to keep a close eye on the decks this day to ensure she was not injured. I smiled, then winked at Tarr when I caught him watching me. He made a show of shaking his head, but did not hide his mocking smile well enough.

My heart feeling lighter, even as it beat harder, I climbed back up to my perch.

Chapter 26

I took a musket out of the barrel and made myself comfortable. Little and I would not be needed until we were within a cable's length of the other ship, and I took the time to study her.

Three-masted, with a hull nearly twice the length of *Edelweiss*, she had the high, narrow stern that marked her as Spanish. Even to my eye, fairly experienced now (I had finally left the 'land-crab' epitaph behind me) but still not as knowledgeable as the men who had spent their entire lives at sea; she looked handy. She didn't wallow as many of the larger ships did, but danced from wave to wave as she curved peaks either side of her bow.

Her colors were hauled to her main-masthead and my heart lurched; for a moment I had thought she flew a cross of St George, but no, the red cross was on the diagonal and jagged: the Cross of Burgundy. I smiled at my correct assumption of her nationality.

I glanced above my head. We flew no colors as of yet. I knew from any number of engagements that Tarr would wait until the last second to frustrate his prey. Unsure whether friend or foe, the prize captain would likely be paying more attention to us than the set of his sails, allowing us to catch up in half the time. But this one seemed canny; he set his topgallant, one of the few I'd seen, and I smiled in further appreciation of the ship ahead. Not many had the balance and the skill to fly three sails from a single mast, and I understood why Tarr wanted her.

I braced myself against the maintop as *Edelweiss* changed course from north to west to follow our prey.

She would be hard to catch, running downwind with all that sail, but we were dead astern. If we could just get closer, and she did look to be heavily laden which would work against her in this race for the lives of all aboard, we could steal the very wind from out her sails and claim our prize.

Then, a crash, and I caught my balance.

"She's jettisoning her cargo," Little said, and I glanced up at our newly unfurled blood-red flag—La Jolie Rouge—that shouted our intentions across the sea: Your blood will be spilled. Ask no quarter, none will be granted.

The three-master hardened up and Tarr followed, both decks a heaving mass of men hauling brace and sheet to bring the sails to their new set. We were stealing her wind; she was trying to shake us, but it would take a magician— or a devil—to shake Tarr off her wake.

More barrels littered the waves ahead. I was concerned over their contents until I realized they floated; they were unlikely to be enough to hole our bow on collision.

At a shouted command from below, Little and I readied ourselves for the battle. Our bow cannon fired—a warning shot, well over their bow—a nice illustration that they were well within our range.

I glanced down, but could not see Magdalena. *Good, at*

the very least she's heeded my words. Although I doubted she would remain in safety.

The crew had left sheets and braces to gather at the larboard rail, slamming their blades against the wood and chanting their promises of death and blood. I shivered; even viewed from this ship it was a terrifying spectacle and sound. Each man dripped arms. Pistols draped around necks, knives in hand and sheathed in sashes, plus all manner of deadly instruments found on deck: spikes, clubs and slings.

I glanced back over to the other deck. They were ready to fight, and for a moment I felt sorry for them. They were sailors not warriors, they stood not a chance.

I shifted my gaze to the deck below me and gritted my teeth. There she was, standing just below the hatch. Difficult to see from on deck, but clear to my eyes and Little's. Magdalena.

Chapter 27

The doomed ship fired on us, so close her ball could not miss, and our starboard side exploded into vicious splinters. I winced, seeing blood, but none of my crewmates fell; their wounds not serious enough to keep them from the fight and spoils.

I glanced aft at Magdalena, but she had ducked below out of danger.

"*Sharpe.*"

I muttered an apology to Little, already on his third musket; took aim, lost myself in the sway of the ships and fired, felling one of the gunners.

Edelweiss lurched to larboard as her starboard guns fired simultaneously, and both Little and I cursed. I dropped my recently fired musket as I grabbed for a handhold and Little's shot flew wild.

As the smoke cleared, our men cheered and boarded the stricken ship in a relentless wave of destruction and death. The partridge shot from our cannon had decimated the crew, and the remainder were outnumbered by at least three to one.

Our muskets emptied, Little and I made our own way to

the prize deck, swinging and sliding through the rigging of both ships. I fired a pistol to fell one man waiting for us on deck then, as I landed, an enemy sailor raised his blade to swipe and I stared at him, eyes wide with terror. I did not have time to draw my own cutlass.

A musket ball hit his temple and bounced off, but the impact had been enough to distract him; I drew my blade and sliced his throat. I looked over to *Edelweiss* and saw Magdalena load her sling with another ball and launch it. She glanced over at me and I grinned. Thank God she had joined the fight; she had saved my life.

I pulled my attention back to this deck, now slick with blood. The fight was nearly won, but I spotted one man before me knock Peters to the deck, blood gushing into a puddle around him. The man then raised his pistol and my heart leapt to my throat; he had Uncle Richard in his sights. I jumped at him, my fist connecting with his temple, and he fell overboard. I looked across at Magdalena in triumph, only to recoil from the look of horror on her face.

Chapter 28

I turned my attention back to the melee on deck. I didn't have time to worry about Magdalena at the moment.

A shot came from above and I looked up, then cursed. One of the sharpshooters was still up there, loading another musket.

I took my second pistol—I had two draped around my neck on a silk sash—took careful aim and fired, just as he lifted his eyes from his gun and spotted me. He jerked to the side in panic, then toppled off the maintop platform. His musket clattered harmlessly to the deck, but his quick reflexes had saved the man himself. He'd caught hold of one of the footropes at the top of the mainsail—the ropes on which the topmen stood when handing the sails.

He swung from one to the next until he reached the outside edge, then with a final swing he let go and plummeted into the waves, feet first.

I shook my head in disbelief, I would much prefer death or maiming by steel and lead than by shark and water.

A blur on the edge of my vision shocked me back to my current situation. I had been so busy contemplating the death of the Spanish sharpshooter, I had nearly invited my own.

I brought my hand, still clutching my pistol, up quickly to block a blow from a blade, then parried with my own cutlass and fought off the Spanish sailor. I was well-practiced with a blade by now, and dealt with him quickly. I looked around for my next opponent, then paused, puzzled. The few men who were left standing were voluntarily jumping from the rails. I knew our flag promised no quarter, but in my experience, men still begged for it rather than leap to the terrors of the deep.

I broke into a run to have a look over the side and cursed. There was a boat, into which half a dozen men were scrambling. I grabbed my pistols to reload them, aimed and shot. Aimed and shot again, but to no avail; they were now too far away, even for my marksmanship.

"Sharpe, well done, my boy." Tarr clapped me on the back and I turned to him with a smile. "That bastard nearly had me," he added.

"He won't be causing any more trouble now, Captain."

"Hah, only for the sharks, lad, eh?"

"Hope so, Captain," I said, pointing at the boat.

"Damn and blast it! No survivors. No Spanish bastards left to go bleating to their king with tales!"

"Not a lot we can do about it now, Captain," I said. "They're out of range of small arms."

Tarr glanced at the cold cannon shackled in place. "No ball or powder—they didn't prepare the starboard guns, and *Edelweiss* can't shoot for fear of sinking the prize." He shook his head and looked over the two ships. "We can't give chase, *Edelweiss* is taking on water and we've a lot of work to do to clear all our gear and stow it aboard this one. Then we've to get the prize shipshape again after the fight."

"What about *Edelweiss*?

Tarr shrugged. "You're standing on her decks. Sea'll reclaim the old one, welcome to your new home, boy."

"You're naming her *Edelweiss*, too?"

"Aye, sailors know to fear that name, makes no sense to lose it, boy." He clapped me on the back again and I grimaced. I hated it when he called me boy.

He made to move away, then hesitated. "I saw that woman on deck."

"Aye."

"She's a good shot with a sling."

"Aye, she is that," I said, proud of Magdalena's skill, even though it had naught to do with me. "She saved my life."

Tarr nodded. "That's good, boy, but I don't want to see her on deck in a fight again. It's bad luck."

I opened my mouth to protest, but shut it again at his glare. He pointed to the longboat, now hidden intermittently by the swell. "There's the proof of it, boy."

"But—"

"I don't want to hear it. Your life wouldn't have been at risk if you hadn't been distracted by her. And they wouldn't have got away neither. She's bad luck."

I gritted my teeth in frustration, but knew my uncle well enough to know further argument would be futile.

"Right, you mangy curs, welcome aboard the *Edelweiss*. Get them bodies off our new decks and overboard, and start swaying our cargo across. The old tub's going down, I want everything shiny or useful salved. Get to it!"

The men cheered, their blood still up from the battle, and ran to do my uncle's bidding.

I went in search of Magdalena.

Chapter 29

I quietly closed the cabin door behind me. Magdalena had the gallery of windows flung wide and stood with her back to me, staring out to sea. I took a deep breath, not knowing what to say. *How will she react to the brutality she's witnessed today?* I remembered the look of hatred on her face the last time I'd glimpsed her on deck. She had saved my life, but taken another in doing so. *Does she blame me for making her a killer?*

I walked up to her and put my hands on her shoulders. "Magdalena—"

She whirled round before I could utter another word, her nails scraping my cheek, and I stepped back in shock, putting one hand to my face and holding the other out to fend her off.

"Blast you, woman! What the blazes do you think you're doing?"

"You killed him, you *bastard*. You killed him."

"What? Who?" I asked, bewildered as much by the words as the English profanity from this Spanish señorita. In the past eight months she had exhibited only a basic grasp of English, now she seemed fluent in all aspects of the language.

"*Leo*. My fiancée, you killed him."

I regarded her in incomprehension. *What madness is this?* She raised her arm to strike again and I grasped her wrist, pulled her close so she had no room to kick, and grabbed hold of her other wrist. "What are you talking about?"

"Leo! Remember I told you about him? He sailed for my father. He must be the captain of his own ship now. He was the man you knocked overboard."

"The one who had a pistol aimed at my uncle?"

She nodded, tears flowing so freely she could no longer talk. She sagged in my grasp and I gently lifted her and carried her to the cot against the starboard bulkhead.

She lifted her hands to her face and sobbed. "You killed Leo." The words came out between sobs, unconnected yet creating a terrible truth.

I sat and wrapped my arms around her and held her close. "I'm sorry, Magdalena, I had no idea who he was. He was just a man trying to kill my uncle. I acted to save my uncle's life, just as you acted to save mine."

"That's not true though, is it? *You* attacked that ship, Leo's ship. He'd be alive if you and your blasted uncle hadn't coveted his ship and my papá's cargo!"

"This is what you wanted, Magdalena. Excitement and adventure, remember?"

She glared at me, but I was saved from the ferocity of her reply by Little, who burst through the cabin door.

"Whatcha doing in here? The ship's going down. Get your gear stowed and over to the new 'un, quick sharp!"

He rushed off without waiting for a reply and left the cabin door swinging. It was only then I realized the urgency of the shouts outside and the frenetic activity as stores and belongings were hauled topside. I rushed to my feet and had a quick look out over the stern; we were definitely low in the water and the deck beneath my feet listed.

I hurried back to Magdalena and pulled her to her feet, then pulled out a couple of seachests. "Hurry, put everything in these." We had both accumulated myriad possessions over the months: clothing, gold, trinkets and the like. "We've no time for tears now, we need to get off this ship."

Still sniffing, Magdalena did as she was told; her instinct for her wellbeing was greater than her grief, and I dragged both chests to the hatch ready to be swayed topside. I kept a tight grip of Magdalena's waist and ignored the odd smirk. Although we shared a cabin, my presence there was as guard rather than lover; not that anyone aboard believed that.

I pushed her up the ladder and led the way to the starboard rail. Planks had been braced to bridge the gap between the two vessels and we crossed over to our new home.

The new *Edelweiss* was much larger than the old, and the cabins were on the top deck. I smiled; the airs would be far less noxious than those below.

I opened one of the doors to find my uncle standing in the center of a cabin filled with seachests, charts, weapons and all manner of detritus.

He grunted. "There you are. Get that infernal woman," he stared at Magdalena behind me as he spoke, "stowed in yonder cabin. And keep her out of the way whilst we sort the ships out." He pushed past me, glared at Magdalena again, and strode down the deck, shouting orders as we went.

"What's got his goat?" Magdalena asked. I stared at her

and she met my gaze, her face void of expression.

I led the way to the second cabin and ushered her in, grasped her arms, walked her to the cot and pushed her down to a sitting position, then stood in front of her, hands on my hips as I regarded her. She raised her eyebrows in question.

"What's got his *goat*?" I asked.

"Yes, why is he so unfriendly all of a sudden? Even more than usual, I mean."

I ignored her question. "Magdalena, you are Spanish. In all the time I've known you, since you first came aboard, your English has been basic, to say the least. And now you're using expressions such as 'got his goat'. What is happening here?"

She shrugged and said nothing.

"No, that won't wash anymore. You clearly have a far better command of English than you have led me to believe."

She shrugged again. "Yes, my English is good. But I am alone here—a woman aboard a ship, unwanted by most. Well, unwanted in the way I want to be wanted. Unfortunately I am only wanted in the way I do not want to be wanted."

I stared at her, trying to decipher all the 'wanteds' and still trying to assimilate the fact that this woman, with whom I had lived in close quarters for months and had only conversed in broken English in all that time, was now uttering tongue twisters that, after a little consideration, I realized made perfect sense.

She continued, and I suspected she was amused by my confoundment.

"These men are hunters. *You* are a hunter. You all regard me as prey."

I found my voice. "I do *not* regard you as prey."

"Yes you do. You regard me as *their* prey."

I opened my mouth, then shut it again. Now she was beating me in debate.

"I know what it is to hunt, I hunted the jungle around Panama City as a child with my slingshot. I know prey has to use every advantage at its disposal to outwit a hunter. Understanding the crew's words when they think me ignorant is one of my advantages."

I nodded in understanding, I had done similar when I first joined the ship.

"Please do not destroy my advantage, Henry."

I shook my head. "Your secret is safe with me. But how did you learn?"

"Leo." Her voice hitched with repressed sobs, but she took a deep breath and continued. "His mamá was English. She insisted on teaching him her language and he paid more attention if I was there. She would bribe me with treats—fruits, sweetmeats and the like—so that I would join him rather than taunting him by gaming outside the window." She smiled at the memory. Though silent tears dripped down her face, I did not think she was aware of them. I sat on the cot beside her and rubbed her back.

"Then it became our secret language. Nobody else in Panama could speak it and we drove the other children wild by talking in English. They never found our favorite berry patches, or den. All our secret places were safe."

"And now you're hiding your English to be safe."

She shrugged and smiled. "Excitement and adventure." Her face fell. "And now Leo's dead. I always thought he would be there, you know, when I went home. I always thought we would meet again."

"I'm so sorry, Magdalena. If I had known . . ." I tailed off in the knowledge that I would still have killed him to save the life of my uncle. She rested her head on my shoulder and I put my arm around her properly and lifted my free arm so I completely encircled her in my embrace. I held her tight, her tears soaking my shirt.

She jerked away and I started to apologize, but she interrupted. "You didn't answer my question."

"What question?"

"The captain, what's got his goat?"

I smiled again at the coarse English phrase spoken in Magdalena's breathy Spanish accent, then frowned as I considered my answer.

He has . . . superstitions. He believes women bring bad fortune to a ship."

She grimaced, but I ignored it; she would have to get used to that attitude, and I was surprised she hadn't already done so, what with listening to the crew's unguarded conversations. "We are not officially at war with Spain at present, we should leave no survivors to tell of our attacks, but today a boat got away. He blames you for being aboard."

"A boat got away?"

I nodded.

"So Leo, he may still live?"

I looked into her eyes and thought about my answer, whether to give her hope or dash it, then decided on the gentlemanly thing to do and nodded. "Aye, he may still live."

Chapter 30

"You lie." She spat the words.

I rubbed my face with my hands then shrugged. "You know as well as I do he was injured when he went into the water. The boat got away much later—he would have drowned by then. I'm sorry."

She broke into sobs again, then slapped my face, hard.

"Don't lie to me, *don't* lie to me. It's bad enough you killed him, don't lie about it too!"

I grabbed her arms, yet again restraining her, my patience exhausted. I opened my mouth to berate her. This was a privateer ship. We attacked Spanish interests, and anyone else we fancied, if we thought we could get away with it. But instead of words, my head bent and I pressed my lips to hers. She tried to push me away, then her attempts grew feeble, her lips parted and she returned my kiss.

When we finally broke for air, I started to speak, but she placed her finger to my lips, hushing me. It was just as well, I had no idea what I wanted to say.

I bent my head again and sought out her mouth, her tongue with my own. The kiss was gentle at first, then grew urgent once again. The emotion we had both experienced this day: the battle; the grief; the guilt; it all merged into one. We shared each other's senses and everything melted into a want, a need for each other.

I pulled the shirt she still wore from her breeches, and hauled it over her head—barely breaking the kiss until the material caught her chin and lifted her lips away from mine. I quickly discarded my own shirt and my hands explored her bare skin, caressing her back, shoulders, arms, then moving to her sides. My hands at her waist slid upwards until I was caressing the sides of her breasts. Her breath hitched, then I felt her own hands exploring my shoulders, my arms, my chest.

I broke off and looked into her eyes, a question, did she want this? For answer she stretched her neck until we were once again lip to lip.

I cupped her breasts with my hands, her skin delightfully soft under my rope-worn leathery palms and I groaned. I could not remember the last time I had felt something so smooth and soft.

My thumbs circled her nipples and I gasped as they hardened under my touch. I realized I was losing control. It was too much. I had desired her for too long.

I fumbled at the ties to her breeches and she brushed my clumsy fingers away and deftly untied her knots, then mine.

I pulled her to stand, our lips not parting, and we stepped out of the remainder of our clothes, teeth clashing as we stumbled, the motion of the ship and the heavy beating of our hearts not aiding our balance.

In the back of my mind I realized we had set sail; the old ship had sunk or would soon, and we were on our way. I felt a pang of guilt at shirking the mountain of hard work that was no doubt waiting to be undertaken, then gently laid Magdalena on the cot.

I curled next to her in the narrow space and she shifted to face me, both of us lying on our sides, but it was not my face she was looking at. I grew harder under her direct gaze and ran my hand down her side, over the swell of her hips, then down.

As I explored her, she tensed and I paused, then she relaxed and parted her knees slightly. We both groaned, then I lifted myself up.

"Lie on your back." My voice was hoarse, cracking with need. I could not wait any longer.

I used my knee to nudge her thighs apart. Again she tensed before relaxing and I told myself to be gentle; this was no sailortown doxy, she was not used to this.

I positioned myself and looked into her eyes. One final question, although I doubt if I would have been able to stop had the answer been no. Very carefully, very gently, I pushed. Magdalena's eyes widened—in pain or surprise I did not know—then she closed them.

"Are you well?" I asked.

"Sí."

I carried on. *Gently, gently,* I told myself, but could not heed my own words. Soon, far too soon, I slumped on top of her. After a moment, she pushed me and I rolled to her side, taking my weight from her. She smiled at me, and I stroked her face.

"It will be better next time," I whispered.

"Better?"

"Aye, much better."

Chapter 31

"*Sail oh*," I roared down from my customary place on the maintop. "Two sail—looks like a fight!"

I squinted to make sure I was right in my identification of one of the ships. "*Freyja!*"

Below me, Tarr grabbed his glass and jumped into the ratlins to get a better view. I could hear his curse from my position forty feet above his head.

Two minutes later, Little swung onto my platform. "Cap'n wants you on the quarterdeck, Mr. Sharpe, sir."

I grinned at him, loving the fact that this man who had tried to cheat me now held me in such high regard to necessitate both a mister and a sir.

"Right you are, Little," I said, and slid down the backstay to join my uncle, hardly feeling the burn now.

"That damned Hornigold," Tarr fumed.

"What's wrong?" I was puzzled, Hornigold wasn't doing anything out of order to my mind. We both attacked any ship that caught our fancy. He held a Letter of Marque after all, giving him license to attack almost any ship at sea, so long as it wasn't English.

"*What's wrong?* That's a van Ecken ship! We took her a

year ago! Van Ecken will kill us if he hears of this."

The elder van Ecken had died at sea not eight months ago. It was widely held to have been an accident, although I knew better. And I suspected everyone else did too. Erik van Ecken was even worse than his father, having not an ounce of compassion in his soul. I thought briefly of his wife, Gabriella, then pushed her out of my head. I could not bear to think of her married to that evil scum, but I could do nothing about it—yet.

"Maybe he hasn't recognized the ship?"

"Bollocks. This close to Sayba, flying Dutch colors? The ship could be no one else's. What's that bastard up to? *All hands, clear the decks.*"

I winced as his words became a bellow.

"Ready the bow cannon. Make your course north-north-west," he shouted to the helmsman at the whipstaff below deck.

Our bow nosed to larboard, the sails were adjusted, and we headed directly toward the ongoing battle, the wind with us.

It took Hornigold longer than it should have to notice us, but when he did he fired a warning shot.

"Raise the colors," Tarr yelled. "And shoot back at that mangy cur!"

Our bow cannon boomed, its ball falling short of the warring ships. I realized that Hornigold hadn't recognized us in our new vessel, but surely flying a bloody flag on course for Sayba he would work out who we were? I glanced at Tarr and decided to keep my mouth shut. I had never seen him look so angry. In this mood, one push and he was likely to sink *Freyja* just for the hell of it.

"What's going on?" a feminine voice behind us asked.

"Get back to your cabin, out of the way, woman. We

don't need your ill fortune on deck now."

I glared at Tarr, then turned to Magdalena and nodded toward her, indicating with my eyes for her to go back inside. Thank heaven she understood.

Freyja did nothing, and I could just imagine the confusion aboard her decks. Then she fired another broadside at the Dutch ship and I sighed in relief.

We drew closer and Tarr ordered the helmsman to bear up to starboard until our larboard side faced the battle.

"*Ready the guns.*"

"Er, which ship are we aiming for, Cap'n?" Gun Master Prince asked.

"I don't bloody care, just fire at them! That Dutch ship cannot be allowed to sail on, and if Hornigold is sunk as well, it's his own blasted fault."

"Aye, aye, Cap'n."

Within seconds, the gunports below us were opened and two stories of muzzles hauled out and aimed at the warring ships.

"*Fire.*"

The cacophony of a dozen cannon going off deafened me and, when the smoke cleared, I reckoned both ships had been hit.

"*Reload.*"

Freyja ceased fire on the Dutch ship and bore off to circle away.

"Get us broadside onto that prize. On my mark . . ."

We were sailing at a right angle to the two ships, just passing the prize's bows.

"Steady . . . steady . . . *Now.* Hard to larboard!"

Edelweiss swung around and men hauled on sheet and brace to keep the wind in our sails and the ship powering toward our prey.

"Make ready on the guns . . . *Fire*."

Again, a dozen great guns fired. This time, when the sulfurous airs had cleared, the prize was already low in the water.

"She's going down, make chase on *Freyja*. Make your course due west."

Chapter 32

"*Ready guns.*"

The crew stared at their captain.

"What are you waiting for? Jump to it, you lazy curs!"

"Uh . . . Captain."

Tarr turned and glared at me.

"They've fought alongside those men." No reaction, I tried again. "Your argument is with Hornigold, not the crew."

Tarr clenched his fists, released and clenched again, his knuckles white.

"We'll only fire if he fires on us," he said eventually. "Now, ready those guns, damn you."

The crew jumped to their tasks, hauling in cannon, sponging, reloading and finally heaving them back to their firing positions.

Freyja swung round and Tarr followed suit until both ships were sailing toward each other. I held my breath. On our current course, *Freyja* would pass by fifty yards to starboard. In a few moments we would be in range.

Tarr stood in the middle of the quarterdeck, legs apart, arms akimbo. I glanced at him; with his bright-red frockcoat, his hat, and the bloody flag above, surely Hornigold would recognize us. He came on, his own board bristling with gun muzzles.

"Gunner Prince, fire warning shot."

The decks were deathly silent, the crew exchanging glances and raised eyebrows. Not one man began the battle chant. Not one man brought his personal arms to bear.

The bow cannon boomed and *Freyja's* outer jib split. I held my breath.

I glanced at my uncle and the hard expression set on his face and for a fleeting moment felt pity for Hornigold and the Freyjamen.

"He's struck his colors!"

A cheer—more of reprieve than celebration—rang out and I sighed as I watched Hornigold's bloody flag sink to the deck. His guns were drawn in and the relief on *Edelweiss's* deck was palpable.

I risked another glance at Tarr. He looked disappointed.

"Bring us alongside. Sharpe, Little, Prince, Dupont, Fitzroy, Grosvenor, Fortescue, prepare to board. Blake, you keep these guns trained on that slimy bastard—I don't trust him an inch."

Hornigold, perspiring through his shirt, awaited us on the quarterdeck, flanked by Cheval and Neville, his crew milling about and trying to appear unperturbed by the showdown between the captains.

I stepped up smartly from the longboat to ship and stood beside my uncle, hands at my belt, loaded pistols slung around my neck. I had to hurry to keep up with him as he strode aft to confront Hornigold.

"What by the gods of Hades did you think you were

doing? That was van Ecken's ship!"

Hornigold shrugged. "She was heavily laden."

"What does that matter? Is your head that addled? Nobody crosses van Ecken and lives—he's a madman!"

"There were no survivors, if you hadn't joined us nobody would have known."

"No, just every damned sailor on this deck—each of whom only need a couple of pints of rum to loosen their tongues!"

Hornigold surveyed the deck then brought his eyes back up to meet Tarr's. "My men are loyal to me."

"Then they are fools!"

I glanced around at the angry faces of insulted men and inwardly winced. My eyes met those of Cheval and I squared my shoulders under his mocking gaze.

"I should flay you alive and string you up to the mainyards for the seabirds to feast. You're a bumbling fool and you've put every life on this deck at risk for your greed."

Tarr's face matched his frockcoat, his eyes bulged and spittle flew with each word. I had never seen a man so angry.

The men surrounding us shifted at Tarr's words, exchanging uneasy glances. Hornigold looked round at them and not one met his eye.

"You were instructed by van Ecken to sail with me—under *my* command. You've mutinied. You know what that means—keelhauling."

Hornigold crumbled. He knew as well as every other man aboard that no one survived being dragged under the ship aft to stern. Flesh ripped open by barnacles was an easy meal for the ever-present sharks; it was a blessing to drown. But he wasn't giving up yet.

"No. Morgan appointed me, Captain. I answer only to him."

"Aye," his men chorused, finally in support of their captain.

I thought Tarr would burst; his whole body clenched in his efforts to retain control. But Hornigold was right. Tarr sailed for van Ecken; Hornigold sailed for Henry Morgan. And no man in his right mind crossed Morgan, even if he was in his dotage.

"Very well. But *Freyja was* put under my command. Welcome your new quartermaster, my nephew, Sharpe."

"What?" Hornigold was startled.

"*Non*," Cheval protested, then quietened at a glare from Tarr. I kept my own lips sealed.

"I will also be changing your crew—half your men will sail aboard *Edelweiss* and I'll replace them with my own men. I'll leave it to you and Sharpe as to who stays."

Hornigold opened his mouth, but no words emerged. He cast his eyes to the deck, deflated of all protest. He knew he was getting off lightly. He may be under Morgan's protection; but Morgan wasn't here.

I glared at Tarr. Yes, I had received a promotion, but I did not want to sail with Hornigold. And what of Magdalena? My eyes narrowed as I realized he had neatly maneuvered his bad luck charm off his own decks.

Chapter 33

"Bear off, Cheval, we're supposed to be running with the wind."

He scowled at me and adjusted the tiller until the wind was due astern. I smiled. Hornigold was in his cabin making up the log. I had command of *Freyja*; and of Cheval.

I curled my arm around Magdalena's waist, knowing it would inflame Cheval further, then stroked her cheek, wishing we could retire immediately to our cabin, but knowing that was impossible while I had the quarterdeck. All thoughts of Cheval had fled my head.

I watched Magdalena retreat, skirts swishing, a sound and sight wholly incongruous to a privateer deck.

My grin turned to a grimace as I caught the sight of the boom heading toward my head. I dived to the deck to avoid being knocked overboard, but was not quick enough.

The sound of Magdalena's scream accompanied the burst of blackness and stars that thrust through my skull.

"Henry, *Henry*. Can you hear me?"
I tried to open my eyes, but they seemed glued together.

A cool dampness swept across them, my forehead, and my face. I tried again, but could only see blurred shapes.

I shut my eyes and squeezed them tight, then tried to re-open them. Blurry images confronted me. A brown haze—*the deckhead? Am I below decks? How did I get here?*

Then a pale orb floating before the brown.

I tried to concentrate, to focus. *What's that? Where am I? What happened?*

"Henry?"

I blinked, painfully, and the orb took on the features of a face. I continued to blink until I could recognize it.

"Magdalena?"

She threw herself on me, her words indistinguishable through her tears.

"What happened? What's wrong with my eyes?"

Another voice, a man's voice. "We caught a bad windshift. Cheval could do nothing. You were in the wrong place at the wrong time, the boom caught you in the face."

The memories came back to me: the quarterdeck; Magdalena's kiss; Cheval's smirk. Then the wooden spar swinging toward me; diving to the deck to avoid it. It seemed I had not been successful.

I put my hand to my face, but it was caught by a pale, dainty one.

"Henry, don't," Magdalena said, pulling my hand away.

"Why, what is it?"

No answer.

"What's wrong with my face?" I bellowed.

Magdalena sobbed.

After a moment, I heard Little's voice. "Quartermaster. Sharpe. Henry." My heart iced as he fought to find the correct moniker.

"Just tell me."

"You caught the boom full in your face. Thank God you were not knocked overboard."

"*Tell me,*" I shouted in frustration.

"Your nose—is broken. Maybe your cheekbone too. And your eye . . ."

I waited; he did not continue. I shook Magdalena's grip away and put my hand to my face. Over my right eye, I could see it. Indistinct and blurred, but I could see it. I moved my fingers across to the other side of my face. I could still see, but only my thumb and the tips of my fingers. I moved it back to my right, my left, right, left, right, left . . .

"Henry, I'm sorry." Magdalena's voice. "Your left eye is lost. I'm so sorry." She collapsed into sobs, draping herself across my chest. I made no move to comfort her.

My eye? My left eye? Gone? I shuddered. *I'm a sharpshooter and lookout, how can I do either now?*

I stared up at the deckhead with my one eye, the beams slowly—ever so slowly—taking shape before me. *How will I survive now? How will I survive aboard ship, in the Caribbees, with only one eye?*

Chapter 34

I winced at the glare of bright light in my remaining eye. "Shut the blasted door!" I roared.

A swish of skirts announced my visitor. *Why would she not leave me be?*

She crossed to the stern gallery and tugged hard on the coverings I'd nailed to the wood.

"Damn and blast it, woman! Leave me be."

"Goddammit, Henry, you're not blind. You've lost an eye, yes, but only the one. Yet you sit in the dark and won't have candle or lantern lit. Enough."

I rose, grabbed the window coverings, and tore them from her grasp. I began the laborious task of hooking them on the nails by feel, the Caribbee sun so harsh on my eye it was squinted almost closed.

"You've sat in the dark a sennight. If you don't let light to your eye you'll lose the sight in that one too and spend the rest of your life in gloom."

I found another nail with my fingers, forced the cloth onto it and made no reply. I worked in silence and turned to her—just as a lantern flared into life.

"*Magdalena*. Devil's bones, woman, douse that light!"

She stood before the lantern, which at least dimmed its flare, but I would not be able to reach it without assaulting her. As I considered my options, she held something out to me. I stared. Well, half-stared.

"Cheval is out on those decks, prancing and swaggering. He loves that you've shut yourself away, he's calling you the sequestered quartermaster. You've become a joke." She proffered the object once more. "Take it, put it on."

I reached my hand and brushed my fingers against it. It was soft; velvet.

"It's an eyepatch. I took a scrap from the inside cuff of your frockcoat so they'll match. I think you'll look quite distinguished."

"Distinguished? Bah. I'll look like a blind cripple!"

"Oh, Madre de Dios. For the love of God, you're aboard a pirate ship! There's barely a man on that deck who isn't missing some part of his anatomy—and not one of them can carry off a patch or a hook or a pegleg the way you can. Now put it on!"

"Privateer."

"What?"

"Privateer ship, not pirate."

"Put. It. On."

Her words were issued through gritted teeth and I meekly took the scrap of material from her, the image of Cheval enjoying my plight finally calming me.

I fumbled with the ties, finding it difficult to guide my fingers until Magdalena took it from me and tied it around my head. Then she lifted my wig into place, made a small adjustment, and nodded.

"Do you want to see?"

I didn't have to be able to focus on her to know the words had been issued with an eyebrow raised in challenge.

For answer, I turned back to the window and tore down the curtains I had struggled to replace, blinked in the glare a few times and wiped tears from my cheeks. I stared at the moisture on my hand. My lost eye was still crying.

When I was ready, I turned and took the looking glass Magdalena held out to me. I stared for a while, trying to make sense of the image before me, then the lines and shapes became clear, the fuzziness lifted and I stared into my new face. I looked up at Magdalena and kissed her. "It'll do until I can fashion a leather one," I said, paused, then asked, "Prancing and swaggering?"

"Prancing and swaggering," she confirmed with a small smile.

"I'd best do something about that."

I crossed to the door, opened it and stepped into the Caribbean sun.

Chapter 35

The quarterdeck hushed as I strode onto it, the crews pausing in their tasks to stare. I resisted the urge to put my hand to my face and adjust the velvet eyepatch, and straightened my back instead.

"Captain." I greeted Hornigold with a nod. He dipped his own head in acknowledgement but uttered not a word.

I heard a rustle behind me and knew Magdalena was at my back, and I was grateful she was letting me take the lead in front of the men after her forceful ejection of me from the cabin.

I continued forward, my eye fixed on Cheval. He had not noticed my reappearance, nor the anxious glances his audience shot my way as the Frenchman doubled up, clutching his face—no doubt re-enacting my "accident" for the benefit of his fellows.

He fell to the deck in parody then silenced on noticing me. I drew my cutlass and directed it toward his throat.

"On your feet, Cheval. You and I have a score to reckon. I demand restitution."

He scrabbled upright, clumsy but quick, and glanced about him, but his mates had melted back at the glimpse of steel.

The Frenchman raised his hands as if to ward me off and I gestured for him to raise them further—his left hand was far too close to the hilt of his own cutlass for my liking.

"It was accident," he whined. "*Accident.*"

I grimaced at the deterioration of his English, something that always marked his play-acting portrayal of a victim.

"That was no accident, Cheval, and you know it as well as I. I intend to make reparation for the injury you have occasioned."

"Reparation? What is *reparation*? I no understand."

"You understand all too well, you scurvy French dog. Reparation—recompense—vengeance—making good a loss. You cost me an eye, I will take both of yours as my price!"

I made to lunge forward, the tip of my blade mere inches from his face and was halted by Hornigold's shout of, "*Sharpe.*"

I took my time to turn to him, instead smirking at Cheval backing away from me, his blade now drawn.

"Captain," I acknowledged.

"You know the law, Sharpe, you signed the articles. Any grievances to be settled ashore, not aboard. I'm not having the two of you cutting up my decks and rigging while you chase each other round like rats in a barrel."

I forced my jaw to relax, then nodded.

"Very well. A duel, with pistols, ashore. Make for land, Captain, this vessel will not sail smoothly until this is settled."

"Ah. What good will you be in a duel? You've only the one eye, you'll not be able to see me, never mind shoot me!"

I advanced toward him, my blade still threatening. "Even blindfolded I can shoot better than you, dog." I spat in his face. "Nothing's wrong with *my* aim, how's yours?"

Silence.

Slowly, I sheathed my blade, nodded to Hornigold—although I did not miss the expression of alarm on his face—proffered my arm to Magdalena and sauntered back to the cabin.

"Can you really shoot better blindfolded than he can?"

"I'll have to by the time we go ashore, Magdalena, I'll have to. Fetch me as many pistols as you can find, I have to sharpen my skills before I truly find my aim like this."

Her face paled and I squeezed her arm. "That French weasel will *not* get the better of Henry Sharpe. I promise you that."

Chapter 36

"*Land oh.*"

"Henry." Magdalena shook me awake. "Henry, it's time."

I grunted and rolled over, hoping she would think me still asleep. I stared at the planks of the bulkhead, my eye focusing on the knots in the wood, and considered the day ahead.

I had spent the past three days in the cabin, throwing empty casks and other jetsam off the stern for target practice. My aim was not true. I was not the man I had once been. I had very little chance of hitting Cheval with lead ball, but even less at beating him by sword. I would not win this duel. Not with only half my sight.

"Henry," Magdalena called again, pulling me over to my back.

"Calm yourself, Magdalena, I'm awake."

She looked at me for a moment and my heart missed a beat at the fear I saw in her eyes. "Are you ready?"

I pulled my face into a smile. "As ready as I'll ever be." I tried to immerse my words in confidence, but immediately realized I had fooled neither her nor myself.

"You can do this, Henry. You will win, you have to." She bent to kiss me and I savored the feel of her lips, the taste of her tongue. This may be the last time I would hold her in my arms.

I grew aware of wetness on my face and could not tell if the tear was hers or mine. I pulled away from her embrace and climbed out of the cot, my back to her. "This is not goodbye, stop that sniveling. I need all my wits about me this morn."

I heard the breath catch in a sob in her throat, but refused to turn or offer her comfort. I pulled on my breeches and tied them around my waist, then pulled a clean shirt over my head.

I turned to pick up my frockcoat and paused. I thrust my arms into the proffered sleeves and allowed Magdalena to arrange it over my shoulders and fuss with my collar.

I spun round and pulled her harshly into my arms, burying my face in her hair. This time there was no doubt as to the proprietor of the tears on my cheek. I pulled away and caressed her jaw. "Magdalena . . ."

"Hush. Tell me once it's all over."

"But—"

She pressed fingers to my lips and shook her head with a small smile. "I love you, Henry."

"And I you." I drew her close again, then gathered my wits and let go.

She passed me my eyepatch and wig and I arranged each perfectly before taking a deep breath and letting it whoosh out of me.

My eye drew back to Magdalena and I opened my mouth to speak but could find no words. She nodded in understanding then motioned toward the door. "It's time."

I raised my hand and clasped hers briefly, then turned and walked out to the deck.

Hornigold's face was almost comical in the speed it fell when he saw me.

I raised my eyebrows at him. "You seem surprised to see me on deck, Captain. Did you expect me to renege?"

He recovered his senses. "No one would blame you if you did, Sharpe. No one in his right mind would challenge another to a duel with your particular—misfortune—still so fresh. You would not lose face if you backed out."

"I have lost enough of my face to that cove. This duel goes ahead. Where are the boats?"

"Ashore. They'll pull back to *Freyja* shortly."

I nodded and walked to the rail to have a look at the sand. I wondered if it was about to become my grave. It looked like any other in this godforsaken sea. Two of *Freyja's* three boats were pushing out through the surf. One of them would be my hearse.

I grew aware of Magdalena standing beside me but she said nothing. Her presence so close was all I needed.

The first boat bumped against the hull and I finally turned to her. "You stay aboard *Freyja*."

"*No*. Henry, I want to be with you!"

"I cannot be distracted and I will not have you witness my death. You stay aboard *Freyja*."

Her mouth opened, closed, opened again before she snapped it shut, gritted her teeth and nodded. I gave her a curt nod in return then made my way to the gate in the rail and climbed down to the boat. Little nodded at me in greeting, but no man spoke and we headed out through the waves to the beach in silence.

I turned, once, to catch Magdalena's eye, raised my arm in a wave, then focused my attention ahead.

Chapter 37

I waded through the surf, the chatter on the beach diminishing as I approached the huddle of men. A number of them nodded to me or grasped my arm in a show of support. Others looked away.

I took a deep breath; even the air felt tense. As one, the crew drifted up the beach and formed two lines about twenty yards apart. I took my place at one end of the space left between them and waited for Cheval. No doubt he had a big entrance planned. I squared my shoulders and lifted my chin high. No matter what occurred here today, I would meet my death with courage and pride. I could do nothing about the pounding of my heart, so concentrated on my breathing; keeping it measured and deep. I would not show Cheval or any member of this crew an ounce of fear.

My nerves turned to irritation as the men grew restless. Coin changed hands and their whispers grew loud enough for me to realize that they were not wagering on my death, but on Cheval's absence.

I cleared my throat, praying my nerves would not tell in my voice. "Put me down for a sovereign, Little, Cheval's liver is too yellow for this."

"Aye, aye, Quartermaster Sharpe, that I'll do with pleasure."

The men roared with laughter and their formerly rigid line began to blur and disperse.

I turned to glance at Hornigold. He stood arms akimbo, staring at me, a smirk on his face, and I knew Cheval had gone. I remembered there had only been two boats ferrying the last of the crew ashore; Hornigold had given the third to Cheval. I staggered as my legs trembled and a strong arm checked my stumble.

"It appears this is your day after all, Sharpe," Little whispered in my ear before clouting my shoulder. I could only nod in response. Cheval had run.

"What the Devil's going on here?"

I turned in surprise at Tarr's voice and spotted *Edelweiss* at anchor near *Freyja*.

"And what the Devil's happened to your eye, boy?"

I glanced at Hornigold, who had turned pale, his black bushy eyebrows even more out of place against milky skin.

Tarr rushed at him, fist flying, and knocked him to the sand. What in Hell have you done to my nephew, Hornigold? I'll have your neck for this."

He swung his fist and Hornigold's nose spurted blood.

"Captain," I called. "It was *Cheval*."

Tarr spat onto Hornigold's bloody face, "Cheval? Nothing that man does is without the approval of this dog." He pulled his arm back again, only for Blake to catch it. "Captain! Tarr," he urged, "let him be, he's the wrong man."

Tarr's physique visibly shrunk and he allowed Blake and Little to pull him away. Hornigold scrambled to his feet, wiping his face with his sleeve.

"'Twas an accident, Tarr, an unlucky windshift on a dead run."

"Hmpf," Tarr grunted, all he needed to convey his disbelief, and Hornigold cast his eyes to the sand in supplication.

"Sharpe, get to my boat, we'll ferry you to *Freyja* to collect your belongings then transfer back to *Edelweiss*."

I nodded and hurried to the water's edge with half a dozen men in tow while Tarr turned back to Hornigold.

"If you cross me again or sail off on your own, I will scour the Carib Sea, sink that blasted tub, and hang you from the yardarm for mutiny."

Hornigold remained staring at the sand and did not react; the calm menace in Tarr's voice having far more impact than his normal rant.

"The rest of you remember that—if your *captain*," he spat the word, "sails off course once more, he will have signed all your death warrants."

The men muttered amongst themselves, but none spoke up.

Tarr leaned into Hornigold again. "Take note of my words, Ed, and heed my orders. If you don't, you had better pray your crew has some sense and throws you overboard before I kill every last man."

Hornigold nodded.

"What was that, man? Speak up!"

"Aye, aye, Captain."

Tarr pressed his lips together, met every eye on the beach, then turned and walked to join me in the boat. I wondered if he realized he had just redeployed Magdalena to his decks.

August 1685

Chapter 38

"Ready the guns."

I hurried out of the cabin, Magdalena right behind me, and cast my eyes to larboard then starboard. A Spanish merchantman, fully laden by the looks of her, was down to leeward, hastily erecting boarding nets, whilst *Freyja* was readying her own guns just off our stern. Hornigold had given us no problems since the debacle on the beach a year ago, and had proved himself a worthy consort—at least for the moment.

"What the—"

I took a deep breath at Tarr's exclamation. I had tried to talk Magdalena out of this, but she could be too damn willful for her own good, never mind mine.

"Get the *hell* out of those clothes, woman."

"I will not sit by in the cabin through another fight, wondering if their next ball will be coming through my wall." She stamped her foot to accentuate her words, but Tarr's color only rose higher.

"You shouldn't even be on this ship, woman! You will *not* be a part of my fight."

"She's an excellent shot, Captain," I ventured, driven to

protect Magdalena from my uncle's scorn. "She can join Little in the tops, I'm not much good up there now."

"The *tops*? A woman in my rigging? Are you out of your mind, man?" He inflicted the full force of his glare onto Magdalena, thrusting a pointed finger at her with every word. "Get back into that cabin and into a gown!" He turned to me. "And you, Sharpe, get up to that maintop. You're a damn sight better shot than you think you are—and you're getting better with every battle." Back to Magdalena. "Are you still here? Get back to that cabin." He thrust his arm out so suddenly Magdalena flinched. "Or I'll heave you overboard myself for your mutiny. See how you get on fighting the sharks."

Magdalena turned and fled. I moved to go after her, but Tarr grabbed my arm. "Oh no you don't, boy. Get aloft!"

Seething at the "boy", I nonetheless hurried over to the ratlins to begin my climb. I had seen Magdalena pause at the cabin door; seen the glare of hate; and knew there would be trouble ahead.

Chapter 39

"I can't stay aboard this blasted ship," Magdalena shouted when I joined her in the cabin after another prize had been successfully taken.

"That uncle of yours hates me. He demeans me at every turn and would prefer I never left this cabin."

I took hold of her shoulders in an attempt to calm her down.

"Hush, Magdalena, calm yourself."

"Calm myself? How can I be calm? I'm naught but a prisoner on this ship! This is not the adventure I had in mind."

I had grown exasperated with her and her arguments. We'd had this discussion many times since we had re-joined *Edelweiss*.

"This is a privateer ship—you know well that women are not made welcome aboard, most of the crew share Tarr's superstition. These men put their very lives in danger every day we're at sea. If not for Tarr and myself, you'd have been used and thrown overboard or worse for bringing bad fortune to these decks."

"What bad fortune? What is it I've caused?" Tears of frustration poured down her cheeks.

"I know well you have done nothing, but every accident, every injury, every problem is laid at your feet. The men need someone to blame for anything that goes wrong."

"And that someone is me?"

"Aye, I'm afraid it is. The safest place for you is in here, out of sight and mind. Many women have met far worse fates on the deck of a ship than sailing in luxury."

"Sailing in luxury? You jest, surely? Bare floors, bare walls, a cot for a bed, and a great gun for company! This is hardly luxury, Henry."

"So what do you suggest? If you don't like it, stay ashore next time we make land—maybe you'll find the adventure you seek there."

"But where would we go? What would we do?"

"We? I made no mention of we. Look at me, Magdalena." I spread my arms wide, displaying my bloodied shirt and torn breeches. "I'm a sailor now. A one-eyed privateer. Shore holds no sanctuary for me now. My place is here, aboard ship. You are welcome to keep my company, but do not forget, you are here of your own volition."

"That's not true." She stamped her foot in her rage. "Hornigold brought me aboard—I did not make my own way here."

"We both know the falsity of that, Magdalena. You said yourself you were looking for adventure, and you thought you could find it here. Well, this is as adventurous as it gets for a woman in the Caribbees—a woman who is not a doxy, at least."

She slapped my face and I put a palm to my stinging cheek, then sighed and sat on the bunk, my head in my hands.

"I have kept you safe from the first day you stepped on *Freyja's* deck. Do you have any idea of what would have befallen you had I not been present?"

She cast her eyes to the floor.

"The only way I can keep you safe is in this cabin away from Tarr and the rest of them."

She sighed and joined me on the cot. "I should never have left Porto Belo."

"No, nor betrayed your fiancé."

She buried her face in her hands. "What have I done? Oh Mother Mary, what have I done?"

I put my arm around her and pulled her close as she sobbed and sighed, tears threatening my own eye. I could think of no solution to this predicament.

September 1685

Chapter 40

"*Sail oh*. Triple-master. Looks a beauty," Little called from the tops.

"Where away?" Blake bellowed from the quarterdeck.

"A deuce of leagues ahead."

"Colors?"

"None."

"Clear the decks. Ready the guns."

"Blake?" Tarr had joined his quartermaster on deck.

"Triple-master ahead, Captain."

"Merchant?"

"Don't know, she's flying no colors."

Tarr frowned. "Well, we'd better see what she's about then, Blake. But show caution, I want to know what we're up against."

"Aye, aye, Captain."

Everyone on deck held their breath as the ship drew closer. The wind blew amidships to each vessel and this was a test of nerve. We still had no idea who or what the other vessel was, but if we could get close enough before hardening up and taking the wind advantage, she would be ours. Trouble was, we could not make our move too soon; she would be at maximum range of our guns, still bow on and a hard target to hit. Also, a change of course too precipitant would mean presenting a larger target of our own larboard to her and make our stern and steering vulnerable should she be heavily armed.

"Dammit!" Tarr and Blake cursed together as the other ship headed up to take the weather gage, and finally showed her colors—a square of black silk. Pirates or fellow privateers. Whoever they were, we had a fight on our hands.

"Bear off, fire when ready," Tarr bellowed as the ship fired all her starboard cannon at us.

I ducked as small ball flew above. *What's going on? Why are they firing partridge shot at our rigging? Surely there could be no advantage in taking our ship as opposed to our plunder. Do they really think we would ask for quarter?*

"What are you still doing on the quarterdeck, Sharpe? Get aloft."

I nodded to Blake and rushed to the ratlins to begin my swarm. I glanced at the cabin door and breathed a sigh of relief. Magdalena had stayed put. This promised to be a close fight; for once I was glad of Tarr's edict that she stayed off deck—however fierce the tantrum later.

I emptied my last musket and had no choice but to reload—there was no room for Billy and his nimble fingers up here with two of us braced on the maintop. I grabbed hold of the mast as *Edelweiss* rocked with the force of another direct hit and shared a glance with Little. Both ships were taking a lot of damage.

"Harden up. *Harden up,* damn you!"

Our course did not change and I glanced astern at the helmsman shrugging his shoulders and shaking his head.

I squinted my eye and spotted a longboat just aft; they must have jammed the rudder.

As I watched, the longboat drew closer again and one of her men stood and hallooed at our stern. My brow furrowed. *Why's he trying to attract attention?* Then my heart plummeted. *Magdalena.*

I dropped the musket I was loading and leaped for the backstay, ignoring Little's shout of "*Sharpe!*"

I landed hard and ran for the cabin, wrenching the door open just in time to see Magdalena's skirts as she jumped from the ledge to the waters below.

"Magdalena! No!" I screamed and rushed to the rail.

She surfaced, spitting water and flailing to stay afloat. Already, *Edelweiss* was leaving her behind; even if I jumped myself, I would not reach her in time and would no doubt drown myself. I screamed, "*Man overboard,*" but no one could hear me over the guns.

Shots rang out above me and I shouted at them to hold their fire, then called Magdalena's name again as she was caught in the disturbed water of our wake and pulled under once more.

A man jumped from our stern and I looked at him, then the transom in surprise. Yes, chocks had been driven in between the rudder and hull. I couldn't think about that, though, and strained my eye to find Magdalena. I called her name again—she was weakening, her saturated gown heavy. The man reached her, and I thanked the Lord he was a swimmer; probably why he'd been chosen to sabotage our rudder.

"Hold your blasted fire, damn you!" I shouted as shots continued to rain down, but no one paid heed and I could only stare aghast as Magdalena was hit time and again. She convulsed and the water around her turned pink. She was gone.

I screamed insults at my crewmates, then shouted again as Uncle Richard fell, his body hitting the rail as he went, nearly taking me with him.

I had no voice left. No words. No nothing. Everybody who meant something to me was dead. My mother and father, Jonesy, Magdalena, now Tarr. I was on my own.

I glared at the longboat, trying to make out the features of the men inside. They were hauling Magdalena in, but it was clear she was gone. The man I had noticed standing in the boat earlier looked furious, berating the other men, and suddenly I knew who he was. Leo Santiago; Magdalena's childhood sweetheart; the man she had run from to look for adventure.

He lived after all and his attempt at rescuing her had resulted in her death. I swore I would avenge her.

Chapter 41

I raced back onto deck. I needed my muskets.

Chaos reigned; Blake screamed orders, but with Tarr newly dead, not many appeared to realize Blake was now their captain.

I climbed to the tops quickly, where Little passed me a loaded musket. He gave me a small nod, but didn't speak. I was grateful, what was there to say? I had just witnessed the murders of my uncle and my lover.

I focused astern to see Blake bodily hauling a man to the rail before forcing him over. *What's he thinking?* The stern was taking a heavy pounding from Santiago's ship and I realized the fate of the unfortunate sailor when Blake forced another to follow. As brutal as it seemed, I realized Blake was doing the only thing he could to save the ship and crew. Without steerage, we were all dead.

I turned my attention to the longboat and fired. Short. They were too far away. Still without a word, Little and I reloaded our cache of muskets. *Edelweiss* was badly damaged. That ship would not just sail away now. This was a fight to the death.

I dropped the last musket I was loading as a cannon

fired and *Edelweiss* shuddered. The gun clattered to the deck and I saw men scattered on the poop deck; far too many remained still. The stern was in pieces—now mere splinters and shards of wood.

Blake stood and stared around him, looking lost.

"We've lost the rudder," I told Little.

"Aye. And that damned ship's wearing round to finish the job."

I glanced up and saw he was right. It took time for a triple-master to turn, even with the wind, but she had no reason to hurry; we weren't going anywhere.

"She's disengaging. Look, she's hardening up again!"

"*What?*" I shared Little's confusion and scanned the horizon. "*Freyja!* It's Hornigold!" I bellowed the news to the deck below, and the remaining crew all but slumped to the deck in relief.

Little and I clasped hands, our mouths stretched wide. For the first time, I was overjoyed to see that scoundrel.

Chapter 42

"So what do you have to say for yourselves?"

Bellies full, the relaxed and somber mood from the dining room broken, Blake, Prince, Hornigold and myself all shifted in our chairs and glanced around the room. No one looked at Erik van Ecken.

"Tarr is dead. He was the only competent one of the lot of you and you allowed him to be killed."

"He was a good captain. A good captain is always to be found in the thick of the fight."

"Shut up, Hornigold. I do not know why you are here. You were Morgan's man, now irrelevant."

"Aye, it's true Morgan has swallowed the anchor . . ." Blake started.

"Swallowed the anchor? What does that mean? Speak English for God's sake!"

Blake took a breath, then tried again. "Morgan is no longer a man of power or influence—in Jamaica or London."

"Exactly. He is nothing, an old man living out his days in comfort and boredom," van Ecken interrupted. "So why is his man here?"

Blake glanced at Hornigold, who was only containing himself with great difficulty.

"Hornigold has proved himself. *Edelweiss* and *Freyja* work well together. If not for Hornigold, *Edelweiss* would have been lost and most if not all of her crew with her."

Van Ecken grunted. "I have been hearing rumors. Rumors that a certain twinmaster flying a red flag has attacked a number of my ships."

"Sailortown is full of rumor, Mijnheer van Ecken," Hornigold replied. "Gossip is a sailor's vice, especially when coupled with rum and the dice." He stared at van Ecken and I could barely believe the audacity of the man. He had no shame when it came to gainsaying.

"Hmpf. Very well, but if I find out there is any truth to the rumor, you will spend your last days in my cage."

Hornigold paled. He had seemingly succeeded in his ploy, but we all knew van Ecken would not hesitate to carry out his threat. We had seen many a man locked in that tiny cage over the years. Unable to move or defend himself as he thirsted and starved to death; his sight taken by birds who did not have the patience to wait for his death before helping themselves to the delicacy; his skin erupting in sores under the unrelenting sun; and tormented by flies.

The silence stretched out until van Ecken felt he had made his point.

"How many men *were* lost?"

"Twenty seven," Blake answered. "Twenty seven, all good men and true."

"And how do you plan to replace them?"

"We will reorganize both Edelweissers and Freyjamen to crew both ships as effectively as possible, then force new topmen and gunners from prizes."

"And how will you control Hornigold?"

Blake glanced nervously at his fellow captain, whose face had flushed bright red at van Ecken's manner. "Hornigold will not cause any problems. He is loyal to me and will sail with Sharpe as his quartermaster."

"*What?* Now wait a minute, Blake . . ."

I glanced at van Ecken; he appeared amused at Hornigold's outburst.

Blake turned to me and raised his eyes to stare at my face. "You are Tarr's nephew, Sharpe, your presence aboard Edelweiss is disruptive. You sail with Hornigold."

I nodded, resigned. I had expected this. Blake did not command the respect Tarr had enjoyed on the deck of *Edelweiss*. Captains were elected by their crews and many of the crew had passed comment that *I* should have succeeded my uncle as captain. Blake knew he had to get rid of me before I garnered enough support to challenge him and take his position.

I was relieved he had chosen this recourse and not sent me overboard during a quiet dog watch.

"Ahh, poor Sharpe, lost his place, his uncle and his whore. Welcome aboard the *Freyja*. And you'll have to be *elected* quartermaster."

Blake quietened Hornigold with, "He will be."

"What do you mean? What's happened to Magdalena?"

The men fell silent and I gasped. *How long had Gabriella been in the room?* I stood and walked over to her. She and Magdalena had met on a number of occasions and, although not natural friends, they had got on well. Probably because each was the only woman the other encountered on a regular basis. Apart from the slaves of course.

"I'm so sorry, Mevrouw van Ecken. I'm afraid she was killed on our last voyage."

"No," she whispered and I caught her as her legs gave way beneath her. "No."

"Get your damned filthy hands off my wife, Sharpe. I've warned you before."

I glanced at van Ecken, sure my contempt for him was clear on my face. He made no move toward his wife and I risked a quick look at Gabriella, pleased to see her small nod before I let her go. She made her unsteady way to a spare seat and van Ecken shouted for Klara, her slave, to tend her.

I retook my own seat, glancing between husband and wife, hardly daring to think about the reality of her life as this man's wife. My gaze lingered a moment on her chest and the amethyst that rested there before van Ecken again claimed my attention.

"You hold far too much interest in my wife than is healthy, Sharpe. You'll bed Klara tonight—that should take your mind off her, eh?" He slapped the African woman's behind, hard.

"You are all guests tonight," he continued. "I'll find bed partners for you all. I have more plans to impart to you, but they'll wait for the morn—and clear heads." He was joined in his laughter by Hornigold and Prince. Blake did not appear amused.

I risked a glance at the women. Gabriella looked horrified, and was in danger of losing her battle with tears. She would not look at me. Klara's gaze was steady: haughty and resigned. I gave her a small smile to reassure her. She did not yet know it, but she would be safer tonight than, no doubt, any other night she had spent in this house. I had already lost everyone I cared about, I would not inflict any suffering on this woman. Her world was cruel enough.

My gaze flickered back to Gabriella, and I realized I did still have someone I cared about.

I shuddered anew at the thought of her married to the

beast that was Erik van Ecken, and I resolved to do anything I could to improve her lot in life. And if I could take my reckoning on Leo Santiago as well, so much the better.

* * * * *

Henry Sharpe's story continues in *Ill Wind* and *Dead Reckoning*, please see Karen's website for more details:
www.karenperkinsauthor.com/valkyrie

For more information on the full range of Karen Perkins' fiction, including links for the main retailer sites and details of her current writing projects, please go to Karen's website:
www.karenperkinsauthor.com/

If you would like to contact Karen and/or join Karen's mailing list to be kept updated with news, upcoming releases and special offers, please go to:
www.karenperkinsauthor.com/contact

Karen Perkins

About the Author

Karen Perkins is the international award-winning and bestselling author of six fiction titles in the Valkyrie Series of Caribbean pirate adventures and the Yorkshire Ghost Stories. All of her fiction has appeared at the top of bestseller lists on both sides of the Atlantic with over 200,000 downloads so far.

Her first Yorkshire Ghosts novel – *The Haunting of Thores-Cross* – is a silver medal winner for European Fiction in the 2015 Independent Publisher Book Awards, and *Dead Reckoning: A Caribbean Pirate Adventure* reached the top 50 in the UK Kindle chart as part of *The Hot Box* set that also included work by international bestselling thriller authors David Leadbeater, John Paul Davis and Steven Bannister.

See more about Karen Perkins, including contact details, on her website:
www.karenperkinsauthor.com

Karen is on Social Media:

Facebook:
www.facebook.com/Yorkshireghosts
www.facebook.com/ValkyrieSeries

Twitter:
@LionheartG

Karen Perkins

Books by Karen Perkins

Yorkshire Ghost Stories

Knight of Betrayal
The Haunting of Thores-Cross

To find out more about the full range of books in the
Yorkshire Ghost Series, including upcoming titles, please
visit:
www.karenperkinsauthor.com/yorkshire-ghosts

Valkyrie Series

Look Sharpe!
Ill Wind
Dead Reckoning

To find out more about the full range of books in the
Valkyrie Series, including upcoming titles, please visit:
www.karenperkinsauthor.com/valkyrie